Moonlight flooded into the little room

It made everything appear unreal. Gemma stood near the table with the matchbox in her hand, ready to light the lamp, but as she struck the match, Blake came up behind her and, stretching out his fingers, extinguished the little flame. Then his arms were around her, and she felt herself caught up against the hard tautness of his body, pressed against him so that for this moment nothing existed but his overwhelming physical attraction. His hands were caressing her skin where the sundress left her shoulders bare, then his face came down to kiss the curve of her neck, and she felt the masculine roughness of his chin on the softness of her throat.

"Lovely Gemma," he breathed.

Books by Gwen Westwood

Harlequin Romances

1333—KEEPER OF THE HEART
1396—BRIGHT WILDERNESS
1463—THE EMERALD CUCKOO
1531—CASTLE OF THE UNICORN
1638—PIRATE OF THE SUN
1716—CITADEL OF SWALLOWS
1843—SWEET ROOTS AND HONEY
1948—ROSS OF SILVER RIDGE
2013—BLOSSOMING GOLD
2081—BRIDE OF BONAMOUR
2363—FORGOTTEN BRIDE
2417—ZULU MOON
2586—SECONDHAND BRIDE

These books may be available at your local bookseller.

For a free catalog listing all titles currently available,
send your name and address to:

Harlequin Reader Service
2504 West Southern Avenue, Tempe, AZ 85282
Canadian address: Stratford, Ontario N5A 6W2

Secondhand Bride

Gwen Westwood

Harlequin Books

TORONTO • NEW YORK • LONDON
AMSTERDAM • PARIS • SYDNEY • HAMBURG
STOCKHOLM • ATHENS • TOKYO • MILAN

Original hardcover edition published in 1983
by Mills & Boon Limited

ISBN 0-373-02586-6

Harlequin Romance first edition November 1983

Copyright © 1983 by Gwen Westwood.
Philippine copyright 1983. Australian copyright 1983.
Cover illustration copyright © 1983 by Fred Oakley.
All rights reserved. Except for use in any review, the reproduction or utilization of this work in whole or in part in any form by any electronic, mechanical or other means, now known or hereafter invented, including xerography, photocopying and recording, or in any information storage or retrieval system, is forbidden without the permission of the publisher, Harlequin Enterprises Limited, 225 Duncan Mill Road, Don Mills, Ontario, Canada M3B 3K9. All the characters in this book have no existence outside the imagination of the author and have no relation whatsoever to anyone bearing the same name or names. They are not even distantly inspired by any individual known or unknown to the author, and all the incidents are pure invention.

The Harlequin trademarks, consisting of the words HARLEQUIN ROMANCE and the portrayal of a Harlequin, are trademarks of Harlequin Enterprises Limited; the portrayal of a Harlequin is registered in the United States Patent and Trademark Office and in the Canada Trade Marks Office.

Printed in U.S.A.

CHAPTER ONE

As Gemma struggled her way down the aisle of the jumbo jet towards her seat in the economy class, one or two people smiled at the young girl with the huge expressive blue eyes and the flyaway red-gold hair. The smiles were kindly, perhaps, but she still felt foolish, hot and flushed after that embarrassing scene at the checkpoint, before she had boarded the aircraft. In her one hand she held the nylon travel bag that had been bought with a view to lightness, but which was anything but lightweight, she reflected, with all the gifts her friends had brought to the airport at the last moment, and under her arm, knocking aside passengers, who were standing to stow their hand luggage, was the offending brown cardboard box that had already caused her so much trouble.

As she tried to put it in the luggage compartment above her seat, noticing with a sinking heart that her co-passengers had already stacked it almost to capacity, a stewardess came to her aid saying, 'If that box is heavy, you'll have to keep it at your feet.'

'No, it's very light. It only has in it a dress, some underwear and a pair of satin shoes.'

'Very well, then,' the stewardess relented. 'But you know you're only supposed to bring one piece of hand luggage on to the plane.'

'I know, but this is special.'

'Not to worry—I'll fit it in somehow.'

'Thank you so much.'

Gemma sank thankfully into the window seat. She probably thinks I'm crazy to bring a large dress box on to the plane, she thought, but it was Bridget who had insisted that she carry it with her.

'It's too precious to go in the hold,' she had said. 'Besides, what would happen if your wedding dress went astray?'

'It wouldn't really bother me if I got married in jeans,' Gemma assured her. 'It's you, my romantic sister, who's responsible for all this finery. I'm going to look pretty foolish if Dion has booked a register office wedding!'

'Not at all. Brides wear the full regalia at a register office too.'

'I'd have felt more comfortable in one of my trousseau dresses.'

'Nonsense! You owe it to Dion to look beautiful on your wedding day. A good thing we're both the same size,' Bridget added, 'No one would dream the dress is secondhand, and in a new country no one will know anyway.'

'No, they won't, I agree.'

'It's not as if you'll have any of our relatives at the wedding. I only wish I could have come with you, but I hardly think they'd have let me on to the plane even if I could have afforded it. I'm too far gone in maternity, aren't I?'

Bridget was very far advanced in her pregnancy. She had married last year.

'I don't mean to sound ungrateful about the wedding dress,' said Gemma. 'It really is dreamy. I can't possibly look as beautiful as you did. It's just that. . . .'

'I know. You don't expect to know anyone else but Dion at your wedding, so you imagine the whole thing taking place between you two, but he's bound to have planned a reception. He's been there for two years, and he must have made lots of friends in that time. What about this Blake Winfield he works for? He'll be there for sure.'

'I expect so, but I rather hope not. To tell you the truth, Bridget, he's the one who worries me,' Gemma confessed. 'He seems to have a terrific influence on Dion. If it hadn't been for him, I'm sure Dion wouldn't have taken up motor racing over there.'

'But that's just a spare-time hobby. You know he used to do it here too—or so he said. You don't have to worry about that, do you? He seems to have settled down well to work on the farm. The photographs of the house look so glamorous, and aren't you lucky to have a cottage provided in the grounds? A wine farm seems so much more romantic than breeding sheep or growing potatoes, doesn't it?'

'Yes, when I met Dion he seemed so restless, but he does seem to be willing to settle down at last. That's why I thought I'd risk going when he asked me.'

'You are taking a bit of a chance,' observed Bridget. 'You haven't seen him for two years, have you?'

'No, but I guess it will work out.'

'Well, it certainly sounds marvellous. I do rather envy you. Here am I stuck in the suburbs with a baby on the way. Your life will be exciting and very different from mine.'

'Not so different,' said Gemma, 'I seem to be heading for the same thing—marriage, possibly children. You know it's what we always agreed we wanted. And you've got it—a husband who loves you and a child to come. It's I who should envy you. Going to the Cape after not knowing each other for very long and being apart for two years does sometimes seem a bit of a leap in the dark.'

'You're not getting cold feet at this late stage, surely? Don't. I'm sure my wedding dress will bring you luck. Just keep it close by you and it'll be a talisman, a good luck charm.'

Some talisman, thought Gemma now, fastening her seatbelt and leaning back her head rather wearily.

The shoes had been the problem. They were beautiful, made of delicate creamy white kid, soft as silk, but at the toes they were ornamented with silver buckles, antique and inscribed with a chased flower motif. When she was going through the checkpoint, the scanner had unerringly picked up the presence of metal in Gemma's dress box, and to her astonishment and embarrassment, there were loud bleeps as the precious parcel travelled through the barrier.

'Sorry, miss, we'll have to see what you have in that large box,' the official told her.

Bewildered, she shook her head.

'But it's only....'

'Sorry, miss—rules of the game. Can you open it now?

And so she had had to open the box that Bridget had so carefully sealed, shaking out the silky folds of the dress, the creamy lace of the veil before revealing the cause of the trouble, the metal buckles on the shoes. There was a murmur of admiration and sympathy from other passengers.

'Sorry, miss. On your way. Only doing my job, you understand,' the Customs official had said rather sheepishly.

And she was left to do up the box as best she could, trying to replace all the sheets of tissue paper that Bridget had put between the folds and to try to replace the sticky tape that seemed to have lost its power on a second using.

But now she hoped it was carefully stowed away above her and would give her no more trouble. She must have been mad to allow Bridget to bully her into carrying it. It should have taken its chance among her other summery garments in the large holdall that had gone into the hold.

She hadn't brought much with her. Dion had said there were good shops in Cape Town. Much better to buy summer garments there where they catered for the sun, rather than try for them at the beginning of the English winter. Besides, she had little money to spare. Dion had kept promising to send her fare and she had waited for a long time in vain, but, when she had almost given up hope, he suddenly sent her a one-way ticket. She hoped he had arranged a date for the wedding as he had said he would. His letters were always so brief, but she knew he was no good at writing. Occasionally she had had a phone call. Goodness knows what that had cost him, except of course he had said he was phoning from Blake's house and she wasn't to worry about it—that employer who seemed in Gemma's imagination to be shadowy but rather menacing. The few letters she had received had mentioned him frequently. Blake does this. Blake doesn't like this. Blake says marriage is for the birds, but not to worry, honey, I'm quite sure you'll charm him once you're here. Blake it was who had revived Dion's interest in motor racing, and Gemma rather wished this had not happened.

'But it won't be for ever,' he had promised in one of his infrequent letters. 'I'm only helping Blake out. Since his uncle died he has to spend more time on the farm, and, take it from me, he's doing a wonderful job there. In the last three months the whole place has been transformed. You mustn't grudge us both a bit of sport.'

Reading between the lines, it appeared to Gemma that Blake had been something of a playboy while his uncle was alive and in charge of the farm. Dion had said that when he first arrived the place was rather a wilderness, but now it appeared that Blake, because he owned the farm, was taking more interest in its upkeep, putting forward all kinds of new schemes. Dion had been lucky to fall in to the work of managing the old neglected vineyards. He had had training in France and Spain, and this fact had recommended him for the job.

His restlessness, his inability to settle in any one country, had made their relationship rather uncertain, mused Gemma, as she gazed out of the porthole at the fantastic pink snow on those peaks far, far below. Could that be the Alps? She felt a strange stir of excitement as it came home to her that she had at last set out on this much longed-for journey.

'You are sure it's not just . . .?'

'Just what?' Gemma had asked her sister, her mouth a little set at her sister's dubious tone when she had announced her intentions.

'I mean you aren't just determined to go to Cape Town because it's a new adventure and the restaurant that you managed folded up and you had to join the ranks of the unemployed?'

'How can you say such a thing? You know Dion and I clicked the moment we met.'

'But that was so long ago. A whirlwind romance that's had time to get stale. You know what people say about holiday love affairs, specially one that started in a glamorous holiday resort in Spain.'

'No, what do they say?'

'That they can't last when you meet in normal everyday life.'

'Oh, Bridget, can't you see it won't be normal everyday life. It'll be a new life, exciting, different,' Gemma protested.

'I hope so,' said Bridget, 'but you know you said yourself that Dion had led a restless life.'

'He's settled down now. After all, he's living in his own country now, and he wants me to go to him. He said so.'

So Bridget had put aside her doubts and swung herself wholeheartedly into advising on the trousseau and finally sacrificing her wedding dress in the cause of romance. The exciting preparations seemed to blur somehow the image of the man she was going to meet, but now, on this long journey, Gemma had time to think of him, trying to get a clearer view of the life into which she was about to launch herself. But it remained pretty hazy. Dion was not good at describing things, or people for that matter.

Now she tried to remember that hectic month in Spain, two long years ago. For so long everything that had happened in those glamorous sunlit days and moonlit nights had been imprinted vividly in her mind, but the edges of the clear picture had become blurred. Now she thought, suppose we'd been lovers, which was what Dion wanted, would we never have parted? Perhaps she had been wrong to refuse him. Heaven knows it had been difficult in those scented languorous blue nights. And yet something had made her hold back. She wanted to be absolutely certain that this was for real, not just a holiday affair. And she had been proved right, surely, for now she was travelling swiftly across the darkened oceans and high above the earth to be the bride of the man with whom she had fallen in love two years ago.

Born in South Africa of a farming family, Dion seemed to have travelled around rather extensively, taking on different kinds of work, never settling for long in any one place. Gemma had met him in Spain when he had just finished some work at a wine farm and he was about to return to South Africa to work in a similar way. It had been hard to part so soon after falling in love. Right until the end she had hoped he would suggest he should go with him, but he seemed uncertain whether he could settle in Cape Town once more, and she had been too proud to suggest that it would be easier for him to remain in one place if she were there.

Everything will work out, she assured herself now as, after the hours of darkness, she lifted the small blind of the porthole and saw a gold and fiery dawn as the sun lifted itself above the dark curve of the earth. He said I should come now that he's managing the farm for Blake since Mr Winfield died. It does seem as if he needs me. Maybe they both needed her, for Dion had suggested that if Blake liked her she might be able to help with some kind of housekeeping in the large old farmhouse. Enclosed in one of Dion's infrequent letters there had been a photograph of the house, and she had thought it enchanting with its deep shaded stoep and graceful white gables. Apparently the cottage in which she and Dion were to make their home was of a similar design on a much smaller scale, with a thatched roof above the white-painted walls with their small-paned windows.

But will Blake like me? Dion seems to think the sun shines out of him. But why do I have this feeling of unreasoning dislike? Could I be jealous? No, that would be absurd. I haven't even met the man. He could be quite different from my impression of him, and what was that impression? How on earth could it be bad, from Dion's glowing references? Was it just that according to Dion he had a poor opinion of marriage? What did that matter anyway? And from whence had she got this impression of a frowning, somewhat arrogant man? From one bad snapshot of a large dark man on a horse frowning into the sun? Forget it, Gemma, she told herself. You're going to marry Dion, not his employer.

In the small cramped washroom of the plane, she made as adequate a toilet as time and space allowed.

The deep sapphire blue of her cord slacks and blouson jacket echoed the blue of her eyes and she had chosen the matching eye-shadow and rose-pink lipstick with care. Somewhere deep inside her nerves were quivering and that sinking sensation could not be put down entirely to the fact that the plane had started its downward descent. But once I see him again, she thought, everything will be as it was before and the time gap will disappear.

Seatbelts were fastened now and far below was the coastline, like a relief map with blue sea and lines of white waves creaming into the rugged shore, then the landing, smooth, hardly registered, and the long wait for luggage, the quick release through Customs, the queue at the Immigration desk to show passports. Gemma went through all this in a haze of excitement. At last—at last she was free to pass through the barriers where friends of passengers were eagerly waiting.

She stood alone in the crowd while all around her people eagerly embraced with exclamations of joy. And then a voice said, 'Is it Gemma?' She swung around eagerly, her arms outstretched, ready to laugh with happiness that now they were together at last. But her hands dropped to her sides. The large man who was gazing down at her with a questioning expression was not Dion. Blake, she thought. Blake Winfield. There, not blurred any more by bad photography, but clearcut and dark yet with the same touch of arrogance, were the features of the man who was Dion's employer. She felt a cold finger touch her heart.

'Dion?' she asked on a rising note of fear. 'Has something happened to him? Why isn't he here?'

'So I was right, although your photograph glamorised the subject a little. They usually do. You're Gemma Maitland?'

'Yes, of course, and you're Blake Winfield, I suppose,' said Gemma. How dared he say her photograph had flattered her? And he hadn't answered her question about Dion.

'Right first time—and as it seems we're to be well

acquainted with each other in future we might as well start on first name terms. Let's make it Blake and Gemma, shall we?'

'All right,' said Gemma, somewhat reluctantly. 'But where's Dion? Has something awful happened?'

Blake smiled. For the first time, thought Gemma. Why should he look so happy at her discomfiture? Furiously she took notes of his appearance, as he towered over her, the golden tan of his skin contrasting with the cream safari suit, the strong column of his throat quivering with ill-suppressed laughter, the green-gold eyes beneath the dark arched brows gleaming with amusement.

'Of course not. Why should you jump to the conclusion that something awful has happened? You'll see Dion all in good time, my dear. Unfortunately he's had to replace me on the race circuit and I had to send him off on the test drive for the race next Saturday. I injured my wrist yesterday and can't take part in it. He sends his apologies and hopes to see you very soon. I guess after two years a couple of hours can't make much difference to you, can it?'

Gemma tried to suppress her disappointment. She wouldn't show this arrogant man that this turn of events had thoroughly upset her.

'I suppose not,' she said, forcing a smile, and then, trying to be polite, 'It was good of you to come yourself.'

'I did think of sending a driver, but I thought I myself might be better able to recognise you from your photograph. Not that I had much time to spare. We're always pretty busy on the farm, as no doubt you'll find out. But Dion assures me that you'll be able to cope with the work.'

What work? thought Gemma, bewildered, but she did not comment. Better leave it to Dion to explain. She wasn't going to admit ignorance of Dion's plans to Blake. He had of course hinted that she might be able to help with the housekeeping. Perhaps that was what Blake meant.

'Is that all your luggage? We'll easily manage that.'

Still wheeling her trolley with its one nylon suitcase, her holdall and the large cardboard box, she found herself being guided out of the airport buildings and across the road towards the busy car park. Blake walked so swiftly that she had hard work keeping up with him and she thought he must be in a tearing hurry to get her to the farm and be rid of her.

'Here we are, then.' He had halted his striding progress and stopped near to a large silver-grey Mercedes. 'Let's stow your bags and we can be on our way. I'm anxious to get back home to find out how Dion has fared.'

'And I'm anxious to get there to meet Dion,' said Gemma.

He hardly seemed to have registered how very disappointed she must feel, she thought. Obviously he had found this whole business of meeting her something of a nuisance. I suppose he would rather have been on the track watching the test, she surmised, and a small niggle of annoyance crept into her mind as she thought that Dion should have dug his heels in and refused to do anything except meet her on this fateful afternoon.

'So you shall, all in good time,' Blake assured her now.

He seized her suitcase, stowing it away in the large compartment, then carelessly took hold of the cardboard box, ready to slam it into the trunk.

'Oh, please be careful with that! It's something special,' Gemma implored him.

He turned towards her as if wondering why she was making such a fuss, and the box, already weakened by the incident with the official at Heathrow, burst open, spilling out its layers of silk and lace. Gemma was able to grab it before it reached the ground and stood clasping it against her.

'Good grief!' Blake exclaimed. 'What's all this, then?'

Gemma felt her cheeks become hot. For the second time she began to fold the silky yards of the skirt with trembling fingers.

'Need you ask? I should have thought that even the

most hardened bachelor looking at this would know what it was.'

'A wedding dress, by Jove,' muttered Blake. 'Aren't you rather jumping the gun, young lady?'

'What do you mean?'

'How long have you two been apart? Two years, isn't it? I would have thought it more sensible to see how you felt about each other first before rushing into matrimony. It's just like a woman to bring an elaborate wedding dress with simply no idea whether she's going to settle here or not. All you can think of is being the centre of attraction on your big day, and not what's to happen afterwards.'

Tears of vexation clouded Gemma's blue eyes.

'I'm not jumping the gun,' she said now. 'It was always our intention to marry.'

'The first I've heard of it. Dion suggested you might be useful on the catering side of our business. We're opening up that side of it to the public. He said he remembered you had some qualifications in that line, and, as you were eager to join him, it seemed like a good idea.'

'That's nonsense!' She said sharply. 'He never suggested anything of this to me. He said I might be able to do a little housekeeping for you, and I'm quite willing to do that after we're married.'

'I can see that at the moment you seem to have a one-track mind,' drawled Blake. 'Everything is centred on that wedding dress.'

'Oh, damn the wedding dress!' Gemma exclaimed forcefully. 'I'm not that keen on it. Anyhow, it isn't really mine. It's my sister's.'

'So. You're a secondhand bride, in fact.'

'If you like to put it that way. But I'm grateful to my sister for lending me the dress, and if I can look as gorgeous as she did on my wedding day, I'll be happy.'

'Always provided you have a wedding day,' said Blake.

'I'm sure I shall,' Gemma asserted.

'And let me tell you, if you marry a racing driver, you'll find you have to take second place on quite a few occasions.'

'So it seems,' said Gemma.

By this time he had taken the wheel of the large sleek car and they were heading towards mountains the colour of amethysts under the blazing blue of the sky. She was determined she would not let this discourteous stranger spoil her joy in actually having arrived. She sat back in the comfortable passenger seat with its silver-grey upholstery and looked around her at the high blue mountains, clothed on their flanks with leafy trees, the vineyards growing right up to the road and stretching into the distance even on the lower slopes. Her heart grew light again as she gazed at the beauty of the swiftly passing scene, and she did not mind that Blake was silent now, seemingly absorbed in his own thoughts. Not very pleasant thoughts, she surmised, for, although those long brown hands were relaxed on the wheel, the clear-cut, very masculine profile turned towards her looked grim and forbidding. Everything will be all right again when I meet Dion, she told herself. It has to be.

Immersed in her thoughts, she was surprised when Blake brought the car to a halt in front of finely wrought iron gates, supported on each side by white pillars. A small coloured boy ran smiling to open them and then they were driving down an avenue of tall oak trees.

'These trees are three hundred years old, as old or perhaps older than the house itself,' Blake told her.

'They're beautiful,' said Gemma, watching the shafts of sunlight gilding the leaves to gold.

Blake's expression had relaxed somewhat, as if now he was on his own territory he was a happier man.

'Oak trees are very typical of the Cape. Our ancestors very wisely planted them around most of the homesteads, providing shade for their descendants, and thank God, although this estate has had its troubles, nobody ever thought of cutting the oak trees down.'

Now, through the trees, Gemma could see a group of buildings shining white in the sunshine against a backdrop of blue mountains, and as they came nearer she could see the main building, the house itself, with its elegant tall white gable richly ornamented with plaster decoration, brilliant against the darkness of the thatched roof. She temporarily forgot her feelings of annoyance and frustration and exclaimed, 'Oh, how beautiful!'

'Yes, it's been much improved in the last few months since I took over. It had been neglected because of my uncle's state of health, but now I'm in charge I can put into operation all my plans for making the farm a viable proposition again.'

One fault he hasn't got, and that's too much modesty, thought Gemma. He certainly seems to have a high opinion of himself!

In front of the house were stone pillars supporting an aged vine and there were steps up to the strong yellow-wood door with its heavy metal hasps. The entrance led straight into a beautifully proportioned room that ran the whole length of the house from front to back with doors leading off from both sides. Gemma had a quick impression of beautiful furniture in light and dark shining wood, blue and white china, a long simple table surrounded by chairs with latticed cane backs. A longcase clock gave out a silvery tinkle of a chime and Blake pulled a thick bellpull that hung near the wide stone fireplace with its cast-iron fireback adorned with embossed decorations and the date 1780.

A door at the back of the room opened quietly and a man stood there in a white uniform and wearing a red fez upon his close-cropped head.

'Ah, Shadrac, will you see to taking Miss Maitland's things to the cottage and take a tray of tea as well. I expect, Gemma, you have English tastes.'

The servant, Shadrac, still lingered.

'Yes, Shadrac, what is it? Have you had a message from the race track?'

'Ja, baas. Mr Dion phoned and says he won the heat for today. There's a party tonight and they're all going straight on to the Langouste. He thought you could bring the young lady with you when you go.'

'Good, good, that's splendid news. What do you say,

Gemma? How about a celebration to mark your arrival?'

But it wasn't to mark her arrival, thought Gemma. The celebration was to be for Dion's victory and it was just incidental that she had come on this day. Blake had warned her that she might have to take second place to the racing, but she hadn't thought it would be demonstrated so soon, even before Dion had met her. She had pictured a meeting very different from the one she seemed to be heading for, a meeting of two people where no one else mattered in the world, and now it seemed she was to meet Dion surrounded by others, taken there by a man who seemed determined to thwart her.

'Be back here in about an hour,' he commanded her.

'What do I wear?' she asked.

He smiled that engaging grin that in anyone else she might have found attractive. With those dark arched brows and gold-green eyes alight with laughter, he had a kind of Satanic charm, she admitted to herself, but now she felt annoyed that she had displayed any kind of feminine weakness, asking him a question he obviously thought simple-minded.

'Anything but your wedding dress,' he said. 'Something cool and pretty. We'll probably end the evening at some disco.'

As Gemma followed Shadrac across the lawns to the white-walled cottage in the grounds, she remembered how she had imagined this first evening, just she and Dion dining by candlelight somewhere quiet and romantic. It didn't seem as if this was going to happen, did it? It's all that man's fault, she thought, but everything will be all right again when I meet Dion.

So this was to be her home. There was a picket fence, rather tumbledown, and an archway of honeysuckle climbing over a broken gate. The garden was overgrown with what Gemma took to be weeds, two feet high, and there were rose bushes all tangled up with some kind of convolvulus. Shadrac grinned with a flash of white teeth.

'No time yet for flowers,' he said. 'The baas and Mr

Dion too busy with making wine. Everything get too much grown when old Mr Winfield alive, but now the baas make everything right again.'

'So he told me,' said Gemma drily.

It would be something she could do after they were married, she thought. She could make a garden here, a cottage garden with a patch of grass and wide beds of flowers. But what would grow here? She would have to find out. A wisteria with thick old branches and purple trusses of flowers cascaded down the white walls of the cottage, lending a kind of beauty even though the stone slabs of the patio were cracked and the front door green with age.

'Mr Dion don't spend much time here,' said Shadrac, opening the door for her to enter. 'Just use it for sleeping.'

Gemma tried to quell a feeling of disappointment as she looked around her. When Dion had urged her to come, she had got the impression that he was going to do a lot of work on the place to make it presentable for when she came, but it hardly looked as if he had started. The distemper was stained and old on the walls and there were patches of damp where the rain had come through the thatch. A couple of shabby chairs and an old wooden table were all the furniture in the central living room, and the two rooms on either side of this seemed to house two single beds with thin mattresses and a bedside table and ancient small wardrobe.

When Shadrac had gone to fetch the promised tea, she inspected the kitchen and bathroom, and was dismayed to find a very primitive set-up, an ancient wood stove for cooking, and presumably that heated the water for the old bath which had black patches where the enamel had worn away. Above the bath she noticed an ancient shower for cold water only. A trail of ants was investigating the dripping tap of the washbasin and, in one corner of the bathroom, a huge hairy spider had staked its claim to a home.

Shadrac had placed her bags in the right-hand bedroom and she proceeded to unpack. It's a good thing I didn't bring many clothes, she thought, as she tried to hang her dresses in the narrow wardrobe. Everything smelled musty. I expect Dion thought it would be better to leave things until I came. We'll have fun arranging the cottage together.

She felt somewhat revived by the strong brown tea when it came. There were dry rusks that tasted of cinnamon and, after finding them impossible to eat any other way, she rather doubtfully dunked them into the tea.

'Anyhow, it's hot enough for a cold shower to be refreshing,' she told herself.

Hot enough too for one of her new outfits, a romantic skirt in rosebud print tiered with insertions of lace and worn with a delicate top of the same material, tucked and trimmed with fine cotton lace, the brief bodice held by tiny shoestring straps.

How will I look to Dion? Gemma thought as she peered into the dim mirror. It gave back a flattering reflection of a girl with damp tendrils of red-gold curls and eyes the colour of rain-drenched violets. The tiny tucked fitting bodice revealed shoulders the colour of alabaster and the creamy curves of perfect breasts. But, instead of Dion's half-remembered admiring expression, she had a quick vivid memory of the mockery in Blake's gold-green eyes when she had held the wedding dress against her and, taking a cobwebby stole, she covered her breasts and shoulders.

On the green lawns in front of Bienvenue a sprinkler system was working, throwing up cascades of glittering water, a fountain of shimmering rainbow drops caught in the late sunlight. Above her, white egrets were winging their way home to their nests in the tall poplars beside the pool in front of the house, and ibis, with shimmering breast feathers of purple and green, were digging their curved bills into the softened grass. The sky, vividly blue when she had first arrived, was now a softer shade of lilac. It really is a most beautiful place, she thought. We should be happy here if only ... oh, well, forget it.

Under the leaves of the old vine, upon the patio of

herringbone brick, there were deep luxurious seats, seats in which to relax and lie at full length watching the swallows dart in their arrow-swift flight, forktailed and dark blue against the gold and rose streamers of the setting sun, and Blake was there, stretched supine like a lazy leopard, seeming in no hurry to move.

'Come and sit for a while—plenty of time. You must try some of our wine and get in the right mood for the party.'

Gemma noticed then that a silver bucket held a green bottle and there were long wine glasses, beautifully shaped, upon the white wrought-iron table. But I don't want wine, she thought fretfully. Oh, why doesn't he take me to meet Dion straight away? Why all this delay? As Blake poured the clear pale gold liquid into her glass, she glanced up at his slightly smiling mouth and felt that he was playing with her emotions quite knowingly, teasing her, like a sinewy male cat, its golden-green eyes fixed hypnotically upon an unfortunate mouse. So, she thought, I won't show him that I'm dying with impatience, that all I can think of is my first meeting with Dion, and she accepted the glass of beautiful wine and sipped it as if they had all the time in the world to waste.

The wine was light, refreshing with a hint of fragrance like flowers, yet not too sweet, and, as Gemma sipped it, the blue shadows were lengthening upon the grass and the shadows on the mountains framing the farm had changed from misty blue to indigo. If the man sitting so relaxed beside her had been Dion, she would have been perfectly happy, she thought. But she was to meet him in a different setting. Was that by his own choice, or had Blake manipulated both of them so that they could not meet alone?

'How do you like our wine?' he asked now, topping her glass up, although she had not intended to drink any more.

'It's delicious. Is it actually made here?'

'Yes. It's pretty new, but white wines don't have to be kept for too long. We have all kinds of plans for extending our wine list. We plan to develop the place into a tourist attraction, a place where people can come to buy wine, spend a pleasant day, taste the wine, buy local products like jams, chutneys, cured hams and sausages and cheeses, and have lunch here when they can sample our products. That, of course, is where you come in.'

The wine spilled over the rim of the glass as Gemma turned to look at this man who seemed to be ordering her life without her knowledge.

'You look surprised,' commented Blake. 'Surely Dion told you about our plans for the farm?'

'He said you were keen to improve the farm since your uncle's death, but, apart from the fact that he suggested I should help with some kind of housekeeping, I didn't realise I was expected to have a part in it.'

'Some kind of housekeeping? Well, there you have it, except that you appear to have put the wrong interpretation on what Dion told you.'

'What do you mean?' asked Gemma.

'Of course I don't need another housekeeper. Shadrac does very well in that role, and heaven forbid I should appoint a woman over him.'

'Then what do you want me to do?'

'As I said. Dion told me you were qualified to run a restaurant. If you were doing that in London, you must have been fairly efficient.'

Dion hasn't evidently told him that the restaurant folded, thought Gemma. Well, I'm not admitting it to him. Anyway, it was hardly my fault, but if I told him that, he'd have something sarcastic to say, I guess.

'So?' she queried.

'We're going to encourage tourists to visit the farm. Wine is a long-term thing and we need more instant profit for the time being. They can visit the cellars and we'll sell books of tickets and possibly a glass engraved with the Bienvenue emblem, in return for which they can sample various wines before they're taken around and shown the process of making it. Afterwards we'll serve a cheese and wine lunch under the oaks on the terrace beside the winery. I intend to employ several girls and have a kitchen where old recipes can be produced. How do you feel? Would you be capable of running the show?'

'Certainly it sounds interesting, but Mr Winfield—I mean, Blake, I didn't know anything about these plans. I must talk to Dion first.'

'You'll find he agrees with me. That was the main idea in encouraging you to come here.'

'It couldn't have been the main idea,' Gemma protested.

Blake smiled. How white his teeth were against the dark golden brown of his tanned skin!

'Maybe not your main idea, which seems to have been set on the idea of marriage to the exclusion of all else, but I thought that these days girls wanted to lead their own lives. Surely a girl from London should be more interested in a new type of career rather than marriage?'

'Could be that I might be interested in both, but not until after I've seen Dion—and let me tell you this, Blake, no one can push me into doing something I don't want to do, irrespective of whether it's a career or marriage.'

Gemma looked into his eyes, shining leopard-gold in the darkening shadow of the vine leaves. Her own gaze held his and they seemed to measure each other like two animals in an equal contest. His hand, strong and tanned with a sprinkling of golden hairs upon the back, reached across the table and cupped her chin. Her lashes flickered silkily for a second and then she forced her eyes to stay open once more, staring defiantly into his, noting the black sweep of his long lashes, the strange mingling of gold and green in the iris and the deep dark central pupil. The long brown hand briefly caressed her cheek and outlined the curve of her neck and bare shoulder.

'Quite a girl, aren't you, Gemma? But in spite of your brave words, it seems to me that your heart rules your head. How otherwise could you have come so far obviously with nothing but romance in mind?'

'Because Dion and I are in love with each other,' she cried defiantly. 'You don't seem able to understand.

Surely you must have been in love yourself at some time? Don't you know what it's like?'

She was angry and disturbed by his touch. The strange thrill she was experiencing was surely due to the fact that it was so long since she had allowed a man to touch her. Blake's hand dropped from her shoulder and he turned away frowning.

'Yes, Gemma with the sapphire blue eyes, I have been in love. I do know what it's like, and I do know too that women are fickle and that the fire of love can turn to ashes. Now let's go. We've wasted enough time already.'

And whose fault is that? thought Gemma indignantly.

She followed his swift strides to the silver-grey car and thankfully sank back into the soft cushions. Now at last there was to be some action. This man had kept her too long before meeting Dion. If he was to play such a large part in their future lives, she must get over this feeling of dislike and defiance towards him. He had helped Dion to settle into an apparently stable kind of work, so she should be grateful, and Dion had said he would give up motor racing when she came. As for this other work that had been offered to her . . . it did sound interesting, just the kind of challenge that she would enjoy—but with a different master, she qualified it ruefully.

She glanced at Blake's brown hands upon the wheel and, with a quivering thrill deep inside, remembered how they had felt on the silky peach of her face and the vulnerable curve of her neck just above the small cleft that divided her high breasts. It's because I was thinking of Dion, she told herself firmly. I've been dreaming so much about how it will be when I meet him again that I somehow transferred the dream to Blake. I must be crazy!

As they came into the built-up areas and sped along the roadway high above the city, the air was like warm satin. In the sky far to the west there were still streamers shading from hectic flames through rose to the gentle lilac grey of a dove's breast, but, outlining the streets and circling the harbour, there were patterns of twinkling lights, necklaces of diamonds below them and above the myriad stars of the southern hemisphere gradually showing themselves in the blue velvet of the night sky.

'Is this the way to the racing track?' asked Gemma.

'No, no. The racing is over for today. There's a crowd going on to a small restaurant for a celebration. We sometimes take it over for the evening. They serve good food and wine. If you like seafood, you should be happy there.'

I'll be happy when I can meet Dion, thought Gemma. She was feeling strung up and yet tired after the hours of tension and excitement on the long journey. Nothing had turned out as she had imagined, and the man beside her had added to her troubles.

Now they were in an area that had tall buildings and blocks of apartments on one side and over there on the right there was the sea, dark now but still with creamy tops of waves rolling mysteriously shorewards in the night. They drew up where there were other cars parked beside a small restaurant shut off from the gaze of pedestrians by half curtains upon wooden rings. Above them a red sign winked with neon lights, La Langouste.

Gemma could feel her heart throbbing. To her fevered imagination, it seemed to rival the sound of the sea dashing against the rocks on the other side of the promenade. She drew her stole around her, afraid that Blake would sense her agitation in the quickness of her breath revealed by the low-cut dress.

'Don't be nervous,' said Blake as he handed her from the car.

'I'm not,' she denied sharply, feeling his long brown hand upon her shoulders, guiding her across the few short yards that separated her now from Dion.

'In that case, you're giving a good imitation of it,' Blake told her. 'Those dewdrops on your forehead are rather becoming, but surely they aren't just caused by the heat. Here, take my hanky.'

The perspiration that had sprung on her brow felt ice cold, not hot. Gemma took the white square offered to her and carefully dabbed at it, breathing in a fragrance of some spicy cologne.

'Don't worry, my dear Gemma. If it's any satisfaction to you, you look very beautiful, a wide-eyed pussycat half scared to death.'

'Don't be absurd! I'm not in the least scared,' said Gemma, but she was glad of his strong arm around her as he pushed her into the crowded, noisy room. As they came from out of the darkness, the place seemed to whirl in a kaleidoscope of colour from the bright dresses of the women, their high-pitched voices like the chatter of birds, the men's striped shirts, the bright blue checked tablecloths and the red lampshades on every table.

And at the centre of the crowd, a kind of focal point it seemed for all this liveliness and noise, there was a man with long fair hair and a blond beard. Beneath the beard the man's blue shirt was open to the waist, revealing a gold chain, its pendant tangled in the curling hairs of his chest. Several women surrounded him and he was laughing with them, but he apparently at that moment became aware that Blake and Gemma had arrived. His arm lifted in a lazy gesture. 'Oh, hi!' he said, and then he was walking towards them.

'My dear Gemma,' he said. 'Beautiful as ever!'

Seizing both her hands, he bent his head to greet her, and as she felt his mouth upon hers and the rough texture of his beard, this moment of which she had dreamed for so long turned into a nightmare. She had barely recognised Dion. He had changed so much from the man she had known and loved in Spain. It was as if she were being kissed by a stranger, and one to whom she felt no immediate attraction.

CHAPTER TWO

NERVES, she told herself. I didn't come all this way to be put off by the change in Dion's appearance. I'll get used to it. She was conscious of curious eyes upon her and made a great effort to smile radiantly up at Dion. She was determined she would not show anyone, least of all Dion or Blake, that this meeting had somehow disappointed her.

'Lovely to see you again. How was the trip?'

Dion drew her away from Blake, casually keeping her in a close embrace and leading her towards the table where a dozen people were sitting.

'My long-lost girl-friend from the U.K.,' she heard him say. 'Meet Gemma, who loves me so much she's come to join us, travelling ten thousand miles to be near me.'

'And she's a beauty too. What have you done to deserve it?'

'Are there any more where she came from? Just take a look at that English complexion! They don't make them like that over here.'

It was all lighthearted banter, Gemma told herself, and there was no need to feel confused and ill at ease, but I would have liked to meet him on his own just at first, she thought.

'Sorry I couldn't meet you at the airport, but it was just one of those things. I expect Blake looked after you all right, did he?'

'Yes, Dion, he did, but I was a bit disappointed that you couldn't be there.'

'But now I'm here, Gemma, so we'd better make up for lost time. What are you drinking? Give Gemma some wine, can't you? She has to catch up on her drinking. We've all had a head start.'

Gemma accepted a glass of wine and sat down on the chair that someone had pulled up for her at the crowded table. She had no intention of catching up on the drinking, as Dion had put it, but she took a sip as Dion touched her glass and said, 'To us, my lovely Gemma, just as beautiful as I remember her. What do you say, Blake? Wasn't it worth bringing her here?'

She looked up and caught Blake's dark gaze across on the other side of the table.

'Yes, I must admit she's almost as beautiful as her photograph. She looks like being an attractive hostess for our scheme.'

He turned away and asked the girl at his side to dance. When they had gone, Gemma said quietly,

'Dion, what is all this? You didn't tell me anything about these plans, but Blake seems to have all kinds of ideas about my function in life at the farm.'

Dion shrugged his shoulders.

'Not to worry. Since he inherited the farm, he thinks of nothing else but making it into a viable proposition. Everyone who comes is a potential victim to his schemes. However, if you can find favour with him, well and good. It will benefit both of us in the end.'

'I don't know about finding favour—he doesn't seem overly friendly with me,' Gemma told him.

'That's just his way. He's a charming chap really. I wish I had half his drive and ideas. It's just he's not too keen on women in general, though, take it from me, they're keen enough on him, when he gives them half a chance.'

'Oh, I don't think I could be,' she protested.

'Now come on, Gemma. He's my boss, and you must learn to see which side our bread's buttered if we're to stay here.'

'Yes, I suppose so.'

'But don't let's be so serious on your first day here. Aren't you dying of hunger? Here comes the seafood platter.'

With something of a flourish, a waiter was placing a large dish of seafood upon the table, prawns, langoustines, crayfish, oysters. The heavenly smell of them rose up around the little restaurant. Another waiter came with large white, stiffly laundered bibs and draped them around the guests' necks. Then having placed finger bowls in front of the diners, he withdrew.

'Your first meal here,' said Dion. 'Remember the seafood dinners in Spain? You'll find this even better.'

Oh, yes, she remembered those romantic evenings in Spain, but now it all seemed very long ago.

'That was another world,' she said.

'Different,' said Dion. 'But it's a great life here. You'll find you'll soon settle. Settle? But what am I saying? We want life to be exciting, don't we, Gemma? And "settle" is such a boring word. Anyhow, you'll find life has quite a lot to offer here—I'm sure of it. Now try some of these jumbo prawns. We mustn't let them get cold.'

He proceeded to show her how to get the succulent pale pink meat out of the coral shells. Everyone was eating with their fingers and making a great deal of noise, laughing and joking with each other. The wine was flowing freely around the table in great two-litre flagons, but Gemma carefully guarded her glass. Blake had come back to the table with the lovely blonde girl with whom he had been dancing. Now he seemed full of charm, smiling down at her as if she were the only girl in the world. They proceeded to share a crayfish, feeding each other with pieces of the white meat dunked in a lemon butter sauce.

He didn't really like me, thought Gemma. Certainly he didn't show me much of this charm. Probably because of my connection with Dion. He doesn't approve of a girl with her sights set on marriage. But did she want to marry now? Her first reaction to the sight of Dion had been one of shock, and she felt he had been selfish in putting the race before the important fact of meeting her, but he was so much under Blake's influence he probably couldn't help that. However, now he seemed most attentive. And what had his feelings been on seeing her again? She would have to find that out soon. Have sense, Gemma, she told herself. We haven't seen each other for two years. What did you expect? It will take a little time to feel that togetherness that we had in Spain. I was expecting too much.

Dion seemed to be a popular person, with the people in this party anyway. There was little time for private chat, as one and then another came up to talk to him and be introduced to Gemma. They kept congratulating Dion on his success in the race, and Dion seemed to be in an elated mood on account of his win.

'Come, let's dance, Gemma. I really feel in the mood for celebration tonight—my first important win and the arrival of my best girl all in one day. Can you beat it?'

His brown hand caressed her shoulders as he led her on to the small dance floor. She remembered how his every touch had been thrilling when they danced together in the small restaurant in Spain. So why wasn't this the same? I guess I'm tired, she thought now. Dion was gazing at her with bright blue eyes, eyes that contrasted with the golden beard and waving hair that made him look like an ancient Viking.

'It's good to have you here, my Gemma. Aren't you glad I asked you to come?'

'Yes, Dion, it's lovely to be here, but you won't be doing this racing for very much longer, will you? It's only while Blake is incapacitated, isn't it?'

'Darling one, it's sweet of you to be nervous for me, but never fear. I feel really chuffed about this race today. Blake didn't think I had a hope. He's always so damned puritanical about keeping in proper training, and I'd had something of a party last night too. He wasn't too pleased about that, but the lads insisted I must have a last fling before your arrival—not that we won't have splendid parties together now you've come.'

He hadn't answered her about the racing, Gemma thought, but it would appear like nagging if she pursued the subject. She would return to it later.

Back at the table, Blake discarded his blonde and, rather to her surprise, asked Gemma to dance. The dance with Dion had been jazzy and unromantic, one of those where partners did their own thing and barely touched. Now with Blake the tempo of the music changed and a coloured soul singer supplied a vocal in a voice like deep soft black velvet, a song about love and loneliness and longing, played in darkness except for the gold and silver lights flickering around the ceiling. As if in a dream, Gemma floated into Blake's arms and stayed there, moving slowly, surrounded by drifting shadows of other dancers. The floor was crowded and yet Gemma felt utterly alone with Blake, and, as she looked up at his sensuous lips so close to her own, she felt a fearful kind of attraction towards him, utterly different from anything she had felt for Dion. She could feel his hand burning through the thin material in the small of her back, and his eyes in the darkness had lost their golden gleam and were so black she could not read their expression.

Neither of them spoke. It was as if the music had put them under a spell. I'm lightheaded with tiredness, Gemma thought. That's why none of this seems real. The music stopped and the spell was broken, and Blake was again the man who had disappointed her at the airport because he wasn't Dion.

'Go easy on the wine, Dion,' Blake cautioned. 'You know you have to be fighting fit for the big race on Saturday. You must have a good influence on him, Gemma. This man of yours is inclined to get carried away when it comes to drinking.'

'Not to worry, Blake, you know I'm practically pickled in the stuff by now. That comes of working on wine farms. It hardly affects me.'

'Maybe you think that, but I don't,' said Blake, frowning. 'Keep an eye on him, Gemma, and use your womanly wiles. It's for your own safety that I'm saying this, Dion,' he added. 'Just cut it out for the next couple of days, there's a good chap.'

'If he doubts whether you're fit enough, why has he entered you for the race at all?' Gemma demanded, when Blake had gone elsewhere.

'Well, he's under doctor's orders not to race this Saturday, so naturally I must try to retrieve the family fortunes. There's a five thousand rand prize, and if I win, Blake gets half and I get the other half. How about that? We'll be able to have two weeks in the Seychelles, always provided Blake can spare us.'

'But if you aren't fit?'

'Oh, Blake fusses unduly. He's a perfectionist when it comes to racing. The amount I drink never did anyone any harm. Look at today. We had one hell of a party last night, I came crawling home at three a.m. but I won my race. With Blake's automobile, I can't lose.'

'All the same, I wish you weren't involved with this,' said Gemma.

'It's no more dangerous these days than, say, rugby. Safer, in fact, because I don't risk being bashed by other fellows. I just have to drive a car. It's safe as houses.'

To Gemma, the night seemed to go on and on. They all went on to a disco where there was more room to dance, but Blake did not ask her to dance again. He seemed very involved with the blonde girl Gemma had noticed before. It was two a.m. when the party finally broke up and she saw Blake tucking the blonde into the silver Mercedes. Dion had a rather shabby and ancient M.G. sports car with an open top, and he proceeded to bat it out along the fortunately deserted promenade.

'Alone at last,' he said to her, when finally they had let themselves into his cottage. No sooner were they inside than he caught her into a strong embrace, covering her face with kisses. She felt stifled, half suffocated by his violence, but she managed to get away from him, putting her hands firmly upon his shoulders and restraining him from any further attempt to kiss her.

'No, Dion,' she said. 'It's too soon for passion between us. I want to get to know you all over again. Please let things happen gradually. Two years is a long time, we can't take up just where we left off.'

But I'd thought we could, she said to herself. However, I was wrong.

Dion's hands fell to his sides.

'Forgive me, Gemma. You look so damned beautiful, it's enough to drive any man wild, but you're probably right, and I'm so flaked out after the race and all that wine that I doubt whether I'd be much good to you anyway. *More is n' alter dag*, as they say in Afrikaans. Tomorrow is another day, and Blake has given us the whole day off, so I'll show you some of the Cape and we'll get to know each other again. Right?'

He stumbled in a rather unsure way towards his room, flung himself upon the bed and in a few seconds, as Gemma prepared herself for sleep, she heard soft snoring coming from that direction. What a romantic way to end my first day in Africa! she thought. And yet she was relieved that Dion had given in so easily. It's all a matter of time, she thought. I can't expect to have the same feelings after being away from him for two years. But I thought I would have. What's the matter with me? Have I only been faithful to a dream?

Although she was exhausted after the night on the plane and the long day that had followed, she lay wakeful on her flat, narrow bed for a long time, thoughts whirring around in her head. Even though this place was in the country, it was far from silent. Distant dogs bayed to the stars, a horse out in the pasture whinnied to its companion, and a chorus of crickets kept up a continual shrill song.

It seemed to be the dim hours of the morning when the lights of a car swept over the cottage and she realised that it must be Blake returning from wherever he had gone with his blonde friend. He might dislike women on principle, she thought, but he did not despise their company on occasions. Well, it need not concern her whatever he did. But certainly he's a man with great magnetism, she guessed, or else why did I have that thrilling physical reaction when we danced together? It was just the romantic music and surroundings, but how I wish I could have felt like that about Dion. Tomorrow is another day. Tomorrow will be better, and Dion and I will find each other once more.

In spite of her rather shabby surroundings, when Gemma awoke, the morning seemed beautiful. In the high oaks, doves were fluttering, holding peaceful, bubbling conversations with their mates. Sunlight, shining through the wisteria, made leafy patterns on the old yellow-wood floor. In the other room, Dion was still asleep stretched out full length on his narrow bed and breathing quietly now. Refreshed by a shower in the ancient bathroom, Gemma put on a sun-dress of buttercup yellow, a dress that left her shoulders bare because it was elasticated on the bodice. A short jacket in white, piped with the same colour of yellow, completed the outfit, but already it was too warm for that, and on her feet she wore sandals of a butterscotch shade.

Longing for a cup of tea now, she managed to light a small Primus stove and put a kettle on to boil. We must buy an electric kettle today, she thought, that's for sure. There was coffee, tea and dried milk in a cupboard, but precious little else. How did Dion eat? He didn't seem to keep any supplies here. Surely, knowing she was coming, he might have bought in some groceries. But perhaps he had left it for her to do. She was just pouring the water into an enamel teapot when she felt his hands on her bare shoulders, and started so much that she nearly spilled the scalding water.

'Oh, Dion, you startled me!' she exclaimed.

'Sorry, Gemma love. You'll have to get used to having me around, I guess, because I'm going to be here for quite a time in your life, I hope.'

He was barefoot, that was why she had not heard his approach, and he was wearing only a pair of very brief shorts. His upper torso was deeply tanned with a golden chain upon the blond hairs of his chest. He drew her backwards against him and this intimate contact with his warm flesh somehow embarrassed and disquieted her, but she tried not to show this, nor let him know how much she disliked his hot kisses on her shoulders and neck. This was the man she had come to marry. This was the man of whom she had dreamed for two years. It was absurd that now she should feel prudish with him.

'Aren't you dying for tea, Dion?' she asked now. 'The wine seemed to make me terribly thirsty.'

'Black coffee for me,' said Dion, and proceeded to empty a generous helping of instant grains into his mug.

'What do you have for breakfast?' asked Gemma. 'There doesn't seem to be anything here.'

'Oh, I usually eat at the big house. Blake doesn't

mind, and it's much simpler. One of Shadrac's daughters comes to sweep out here and collects my washing, but the catering is all done in the main kitchen.'

'That's all very well for you—you're employed by him. But what about me? He can't be expected to feed me as well. I'm not working for him, am I?'

'You soon will be. Not to worry, Gemma. Blake's a very generous man. He won't grudge you a plate of eggs and bacon this morning.'

I don't care for this set-up at all, thought Gemma. The idea of having to eat with Blake every day of her life here was not appealing. And Dion seemed to be taking it for granted that she would accept Blake's offer of a job. In fact Blake seemed to be organising their lives. Dion seemed to use the cottage merely as a base and not a very attractive base at that.

'But when we're married. . . .' Gemma said now.

She looked across at Dion where he sat at the old wooden board drinking his coffee, and noticed that he looked away from her, not meeting her eyes.

'When we're married,' she persisted, for after all, she thought, that's the real reason why I came here, 'we'll do up the cottage, won't we? We'll have meals here and lead a life of our own.'

'If that's what you want,' said Dion. 'But, Gemma, it's much less trouble for you to eat at the house. There's always lashings of food there, and when the catering side is started, we can eat under the oaks. You won't have much time for running a house if you're going to take that on. We don't want to have to spend money on food when we can get it all free, and this place is quite adequate. We won't spend much time here. We'll want to travel around Africa when we can, and that takes money too.'

'Oh, very well,' said Gemma.

She didn't want the argument to be about money on her very first day with Dion—but he could have told me about these plans for my working here instead of plunging me in at the deep end like this, she thought.

As it was, Blake had just finished breakfast when

they arrived at the house. He must have been up early in spite of his late arrival home. The meal had been served on the patio on a white wrought iron table, where Gemma had had the wine yesterday. Now honey, marmalade and orange juice, all in sparkling crystal containers, reflected the sun that sparkled through the leaves of the old vine. Blake was sitting looking relaxed, a pottery mug of coffee in his hands, his legs stretched out, the khaki material tight over his thighs, an adoring golden spaniel at his feet. As they ascended the stone steps, Dion put his arm casually around Gemma's bare shoulders in a possessive gesture, and there was something satirical in Blake's dark glance as he greeted them.

'So here you are. Even lovers have to eat some time, don't they, Gemma? And what are your plans for today?'

'Up the cableway to the top of Table Mountain first. The weather looks pretty good—no tablecloth, we'll hope. It's a priority for first-time visitors to Cape Town, don't you agree?'

'Sure, then how about Constantia for lunch, and you can take in Clifton and Llandudno, come back past Kirstenbosch and have tea there if you have time. The proteas should be at their best right now.'

There he goes, organising our lives again! thought Gemma. I must stop this resentment. He's only being kind. Kind? He doesn't actually look as if he's capable of such a thing as kindness. She hadn't liked the remark about lovers. Did he think she would sleep with Dion straight away after two years' absence? Obviously he did. I guess he'd smile in that mocking way if he knew I still am inexperienced in the ultimate kind of lovemaking, she thought. Oh, why did I remain so faithful to the memory of Dion, and now I don't feel the same? Early days yet, she assured herself. Today will change it all.

Presently she found herself left alone with Blake as Dion went to get fuel for the car, and she was conscious again of those gold-green eyes somehow sizing her up.

'I'm glad to see you alone, Gemma,' he said. 'I wanted to speak to you.'

'Yes, Blake?'

Gemma's voice was cool. She could not think what Blake had to say to her, but whatever it was she thought it might be unpleasant.

'I want you to go easy today with Dion.'

Gemma's blue eyes opened in astonished bewilderment.

'How "go easy"?' she asked.

'Don't play the innocent, Gemma. You seem quite an intelligent girl. You look tired out already, so what's it doing to him? Keep a bit of a rein on the lovemaking. I realise it's difficult when you've been apart for two years, but Dion has a very important race to drive tomorrow. It won't do for him to come to it unfit, and it certainly won't do him any good if he's spent the day making love to you.'

Gemma felt her face burning hot.

'So making love doesn't come into the programme you've planned for us!'

He was quite unperturbed by her obvious annoyance.

'Perhaps you could keep a check on it. I'm only asking you to be circumspect until after the race, you understand. And do watch Dion's drinking. He's not quite as tough as he would like to believe when he's drinking wine, and don't let him get on to the hard tack, for heaven's sake. No brandy or gin. If he drinks too much of that, it will spoil his judgment. He never learns, but a hangover is the last thing he needs tomorrow.'

'If you're so doubtful about him, why is he going in the race?' she asked.

'Oh, he's quite a skilful driver if he keeps sober before the race. He's almost up to my standard if nothing goes wrong.'

'But you think you're better?'

'Naturally, but with this wrist we have to be satisfied with second best.'

'Do you know what I think?'

Her blue eyes were dark and fierce as she stared into his own. He looked so terribly superior, she thought, sitting there handing out his unwanted advice.

'I'd be interested to know,' he drawled.

'I think it's a great pity you ever got Dion involved in the racing. Especially if you have all these reservations about him.'

'My good girl, there's nothing wrong with Dion's driving if he just keeps off drink and women up until the race. It's just a pity you came at such an awkward time. I can't think why Dion didn't put it off for a couple of weeks.'

'What you seem to mean is it's a pity I ever came at all,' retorted Gemma.

Blake smiled a slow lazy smile and Gemma's hand itched to hit it from his face.

'Not in the least. I'm hoping your experience will prove useful in my business, and the fact that you're in love with Dion makes it more likely that you'll stay here.'

'The fact that I'm going to marry Dion should please you, then.'

'Not so fast! These days love doesn't necessarily mean marriage. Wouldn't it be wiser to wait a little longer before plunging into matrimony?'

'I'm not with you,' she said. 'One moment you're telling me you want me to stay, and the next you're warning me off.'

'Only warning you off marriage. It's always seemed to me such a final step.'

'Is that why you've never taken it yourself?' she demanded spiritedly.

A frown like a cloud over a sunlit landscape darkened his expression.

'Believe it or not, I did contemplate it once,' he told her.

'You surprise me. What happened to put you off?'

'It's a usual but not very interesting story. Some other time maybe. However, let me make it clear to you. I'm not here to criticise your morals, so take your time over deciding to marry Dion.'

'What you mean is it's all right to sleep with him but not important to marry him. Have I got it right?' she asked coldly.

'Something like that. But I can see that wedding dress even now reflected in the blue of your eyes. I doubt that Dion will stand a chance against the temptation of being the centre of attraction for a day, which is all that women seem to have in mind.'

'Absolute nonsense! You seem to have very antiquated ideas about women. I told my sister I wouldn't mind if I were to marry in jeans.'

'But marriage is definitely the object, and you would prefer the finery you brought with you, however secondhand. Oh, well, I suppose you'll make up your own minds,' Blake shrugged. 'Apart from the fact that I want the business of the farm to run smoothly, it really has little to do with me.'

'No, it hasn't, has it?' said Gemma, rising as Dion came in sight driving the old M.G.

'Have a good day,' said Blake graciously, raising a hand in farewell as they started off.

Gemma stared straight ahead of her, pretending not to notice.

'Why didn't you say goodbye to Blake?' asked Dion as he changed gear with a great sound of roaring.

'He annoys me,' Gemma told him.

'How come?'

'He's been giving me advice, trying to run our lives.'

'Look, honey, you've only just met him. Don't be like that. He's only thinking of our good, whatever he says. And it's been terrific, the way he's got everything going again on the farm. He really has done a magnificent job.'

'I'm tired of hearing how wonderful he's been!' she snapped. 'It doesn't give him the right to interfere in our lives.'

'Tell me more about it later, sweetie. We've got lots to discuss, but right at this moment I have to nurse the car.'

Nurse it, thought Gemma. What a word to use for a snorting scary monster like this one—because Dion was batting it out on the twists and turns of the road as if he were already on the race track.

'Hang on a bit, Dion!' she protested. 'I do want to see a bit of the scenery.'

The view was becoming more exciting as the car climbed higher up the precipitous streets. Houses seemed to hang upon the sides of the roads like nests on a cliff face. Eventually they reached their object, the lower cable station. Even from here the view over the city was magnificent, with its roofs in all styles and colours, faded reds and greens and blues, and the harbour with ships like toys in an oddly shaped swimming bath, and distant cranes looking like giraffes bending over to drink. Soon they were in the bright red cable car, and in a few moments it was travelling at speed up the side of the mountain. The ground dropped away below them and now they were hanging in space, frail travellers with only this small box between themselves and the rocks below.

'It's so extraordinary,' said Gemma, 'to have a mountain like this one overshadowing a city as big as Cape Town.'

'The mountain was here long before the city,' Dion told her.

In the cooler temperature of the mountain, she had need of the jacket. Dion put his arm around her, steadying her in the movement of the car, as they climbed higher and higher now against the huge cliffs that made the flat table top. And then they were there, emerging into a foyer with souvenir displays, all kinds of goods displaying the protea, which is South Africa's national flower.

Dion hastened to take Gemma to a viewpoint from where they could see the city spread in its sunlit beauty below them.

'What a glorious day,' said Gemma, as, discarding her jacket again, she felt the sun glow warm on her bare shoulders.

'We'll have many more like this,' Dion promised. 'But it's unusual to be on top of Table Mountain without wind. Often it blows a gale up here, but this morning the weather has been laid on specially to welcome you. It's good to have you here, Gemma.'

'It's good to be here, Dion,' Gemma replied.

But what's wrong with me? she thought. I'm here at

last after all this time, in this beautiful place with the man I'm supposed to love, but so far we've failed to strike the spark there was between us before. Has he some doubts too? What does he really feel now he's met me again?

If Dion had any doubts, he certainly didn't show them yet as he pointed out the various points of interest in the panorama spread before them, the sprawling city with its old buildings and new blocks of apartments, and beyond it the sea, startlingly blue with there in the middle distance Robben Island, looking beautiful but used as a penal settlement.

'The fairest Cape in all the world, Van Riebeeck called it,' Dion told her. 'How do you feel about making your home here for a while?'

'It all looks gorgeous, but why only for a while?'

Dion laughed.

'You remember me—I believe in living by the day. I don't want to think I'll be here for ever. It suits me very well for the time being, but who knows? When the travel bug bites me, I'll be off on my bicycle again.'

'So you don't feel particularly attached to the Cape?'

'Not any more so than any other part of the country. The world's a big place, Gemma, and there are lots of places I haven't seen yet.'

'Does Blake feel that too?' she asked.

'Oh, Blake ... no, now he's acquired the farm, he's transformed himself into a solid citizen. He's dead keen on making a go of it.'

'He doesn't seem a particularly solid citizen to me. He looks as if he could be a bit wild.'

'Oh, yes, I guess he can give it a whirl if he feels like it, but basically he's obsessed with pulling the farm together.'

'I do wonder how it would be to work for him,' mused Gemma. 'In spite of all you say in his favour, Dion, I think he could be a hard taskmaster, and he doesn't seem to approve of women much.'

'Don't let that worry you. It's all part of a wider story. Some bird let him down. I met her once. She was a dazzler all right—Trina van Zyl—out-of-this-world beautiful. The wedding was all arranged, and then off she flipped with some other guy.'

'Why did she do that?' asked Gemma.

'It was before Blake had inherited the farm. At the time he was a bit wild and seemed to have poor prospects. I guess that was it. She was the rich, spoiled daughter of a business man in the district and she married someone nearer to her kind. It sent Blake into a tailspin, I can tell you.'

'When was all this?'

'About two years ago, just after I came. It seemed to make him a spot bitter in his opinion of women in general. But, Gemma, basically he's a good guy, so don't hold it against him. Now what do you say to walking over to Maclear's Beacon to work up an appetite for our lunch?'

Now Gemma tried to put the thought of Blake from her mind and to concentrate on the present. The top of Table Mountain was rocky and yet covered with vegetation. The walking was easy and the sun warm on their shoulders. There were other people around, so whatever ideas Dion might have had about being alone to make love to Gemma had to be kept in check. She enjoyed the walk, chatting easily to Dion, admiring the extensive views over city and mountain. It was only when he touched her, putting his arm on her bare shoulders, stealing the occasional kiss on the cheek, that she felt that small frisson of distaste, but she told herself she must get over that. It had not been like this before, so it was unfair to Dion to feel like this now.

On the other side of the mountain, when they had followed the signs to the beacon, they were rewarded with glorious views of Hout Bay and the long white sandy beach of Muizenberg far below.

'There are lots of beaches where we can sunbathe and swim around there,' said Dion. 'That's the Indian Ocean side, much warmer than the Atlantic that we saw below us first. The Benguela current brings cold water there from the Arctic. It's surprisingly freezy on the hottest day.'

Inland they could see other mountains, ranges outlined like something in a geography book.

'Hellshoogte and the Helderberg, near Stellenbosch—a pretty little town. We'll go there one day. Now you have come here there are so many things we can do together, if only Blake will let me off the hook sometimes.'

In all their conversation the one thing that Dion had not mentioned was their forthcoming marriage. Gemma found this odd, considering she had thought that was the main purpose of her coming here. Dion had said he would arrange a date and see to the legal side of things before she came, but now he had not told her anything about this.

Although there was a stone tea-room at the top of the mountain, Dion had decided to lunch at the Round House at Kloof Nek amongst the trees above Clifton.

'It was originally an old hunting lodge,' he told Gemma. 'We'll get a light lunch there.'

But although they were lunching on cold meat and salads, he insisted on ordering a whole bottle of wine.

'Do you really think you should have more wine, after last night?' asked Gemma.

Dion pulled a wry face.

'Don't tell me you've turned into a nagging woman, Gemma! No, don't tell me, I can guess. Blake's been talking to you and he's got you on his side.'

'It's not a question of being on his side,' Gemma protested, 'but it seems only sensible to curb the drinking a little if you have this big race tomorrow.'

'Nonsense! Wine never did me any harm. Besides, I expect you to drink half of it.'

But she noticed that he filled his glass more frequently than her own and drank most of the bottle himself, whereas she had just about two half measures. There seemed little she could do about it and it hardly seemed to affect him, certainly, except to loosen his tongue a little. She noticed that his bright blue eyes were a little bloodshot, but that might have been from the effects of the party the night before, the drink combined with the smokiness of the places they had visited.

'Are you pleased with what you see?' he demanded now, having noticed her anxious regard.

'Yes, Dion, I think so, but are you?'

He put one large hand over the table and enclosed hers.

'You're very beautiful, Gemma, more beautiful than I remembered. I'm very glad you've come. We'll have a wonderful time here. As I remember it, you rather put a check on me during that month in Spain, but there's no need for that now, is there, Gemma? You must have grown up a bit since then and had more experience.'

Did he not expect me to be faithful to him, then? thought Gemma.

'I don't know about that,' she said.

'You knew how to put a man off in those days, Gemma, but now you've thrown your cap over the windmill by coming here, isn't that so? Say we can be lovers quite soon, my Gemma. That's what you came for, don't deny it now.'

'I thought I came to marry you,' said Gemma, her face flaming.

'Maybe later, who knows? But nowadays marriage isn't that important to a girl, is it?'

'You too have been listening to Blake,' Gemma accused him.

'Sometimes he speaks sound sense. He doesn't think we should make it a permanent tie yet. He thinks you should see how you settle down first.'

'And you agree with him?'

'Oh, Gemma, you know I'm terribly attracted to you. I want us to live together, with everything that that means, but Blake has something going when he says we should get to know each other better before plunging into marriage. We don't have to have any kind of contract, do we? Marriage can come later if we decide we want a more permanent relationship.'

'So you haven't made any arrangements as you said you would,' said Gemma coldly.

'No, Gemma, I thought you would prefer to let things go for a while until you see how you like the country.'

'You didn't say anything of this when you implored me to come,' she pointed out.

'Of course I wanted you to come. Looking at you, who wouldn't? But Blake is a wise man, wiser than me, I think, and he thinks we should wait.'

'Oh, damn Blake!' exclaimed Gemma vehemently. 'Must we dance to his tune all the time?'

'Steady on, Gemma, if it hadn't been for Blake, I would never have been in a position to send for you. It was when I told him you'd been in the catering trade that he began to show some interest. He thought it would be a good idea for you to come, and it was he who bought your ticket.'

'What?' she gasped.

'Yes, didn't I tell you that? I never seem able to save. Somehow money slips through my fingers, but Blake didn't mind. After all, you are going to work for him, aren't you?'

'I guess I'll have to now. I had no idea I was obliged to him for that.'

'Oh, don't worry. He can spare it now the farm has begun to prosper. He can't spend all his money on racing cars. Incidentally, I signed a sort of contract on your behalf. I told him I was sure you wouldn't mind.'

'I wish you'd explained all this before I came,' Gemma said crossly.

'What's the odds? You always said you were longing to come to see me again. So here we are, and very nice too.'

And you take it for granted that I'm willing to live with you without marriage, Gemma thought. Dion had said they would become lovers, but this was not what Gemma had visualised all those thousands of miles away. I've really burned my boats, she thought. I'm here in a strange land with hardly any money—certainly not enough to pay my return fare. And the man I thought I was going to marry now blithely disowns any idea of it and suggests we should become lovers. And even if he wanted to marry me now, do I want it? I was just faithful to an idea, it seems, not to a living man. And what's to happen when we return tonight to that little cottage? I can't fend him off for ever.

She felt deeply disappointed by his attitude, but all she said was, 'Thank you for being frank, Dion. Now I know where I stand.'

He did not seem to notice her coolness towards him. By this time he was in an expansive mood, owing no doubt to the amount of wine he had drunk.

'Don't worry your head about anything today, Gemma. I intend to show you the Cape and then we'll have a slap-up dinner somewhere nice and quiet. You won't put me off again tonight so easily, I warn you—but then you won't want to, will you?'

CHAPTER THREE

'A SPLENDID day, don't you agree, Gemma love? It's all been absolutely ace!'

Dion's speech came out in a rather slurred way, and Gemma felt worried. What, she asked herself, could she have done about it? What did Blake expect? She had tried to restrain Dion's drinking, but to no purpose. He was obviously used to drinking a lot and laughed off her protests, saying that now she was in South Africa she would have to get used to heavier drinking habits.

'You're in wine country, Gemma my love. Must take advantage of that.'

'But not to excess,' she protested.

'I'm being very circumspect,' he said. 'I've hardly had anything today. You should have been at that party the night before you came—that was some binge all right!'

Now they were back at the cottage, the fresh air seemed to have made him worse instead of better, and she only hoped that he would pass out as he had done the night before, without too much fuss. Well, she had not been able to comply with Blake's demands in one way, for Dion had certainly had more than was good for him in the way of wine and spirits, but her ideas on lovemaking coincided with Blake's and tonight she was only too willing to obey him in this. But Dion had other ideas. As soon as they were back in the cottage, he enfolded her in a bearlike hug.

'Two years is a long time to be apart, Gemma,' he murmured into her neck. 'Do I get my reward tonight for so much patience?'

He could not be said to be patient now, she thought frantically, as he pushed her down upon the hard bed and began to claw at her thin dress, pulling the bodice down from her breasts with a ripping sound. One heavy knee came hurtfully between her thighs and she felt his large hands on the smooth bareness of her legs travelling quickly upwards.

'No!' she cried frantically. 'No, Dion, not now, not like this!'

'What's wrong?' he asked, removing his mouth which was suffocatingly over her own. 'This is what you want. This is what you came for, isn't it? You are in love with me, aren't you?'

'I don't know,' she told him. 'Something has changed. You must give me more time.'

'Time is what we haven't got. I want you now.'

'Dion, you're drunk! Please listen to me. You'll spoil everything if you take me like this, with no joy and against my will.'

'Don't give me that! It's not against your will—you're just playing hard to get. Girls are always like that—or rather nice girls like you. And you are nice, aren't you? Too nice for your own good. But stop talking, Gemma. It's no time for conversation. Take it from me, you're going to enjoy this.'

His mouth came down again and his body pressed heavily on hers. Seeming to gain strength from desperation, she somehow managed to thrust him off and roll away from him on to the floor. No time to think of hurt before she regained her balance. On her feet now, she rushed over to the door, and seizing the key, banged it and locked it from the outside. Ignoring Dion's drunken protests, she ran away into the night. Instinctively she ran towards the big house, glimmering white in the moonlight, but, before she arrived there, she stopped in the shadow of the oaks. She could hear Dion banging on the door, shouting, and she hoped Blake could not hear it from the house, but presently the noise ceased and she could only think hopefully that perhaps he had flung himself on the bed and passed out as he had last night.

But what was she to do now? She dared not face a repetition of the previous scene. Alone in the African night, an enormous golden moon shining down on her, she could not appreciate the beauty of the shimmering landscape, for she felt too desperate. She remembered now that she had noticed a glass conservatory on one side of the house where the patio furniture appeared to be stored against the ravages of the heavy night dew. Would it be locked? She walked towards the house and the only sound was the cry of a curlew from the grassy farmlands and the scrunch of her sandals upon the gravel. Good, it was unlocked. She let herself in quietly and in the moonlight she could see the long reclining chair in which she had seen Blake taking his ease. Utterly exhausted, she lay upon this and considered her situation.

How had her lovely dream turned into a nightmare? Was it her own fault? Had she really imagined the emotions of two years ago? And yet at the same time it had seemed so real. Had she changed, or was it Dion? There had never been a scene like that in her previous acquaintance with him. Had she asked for it, then, appearing to fling herself at his head by coming out all this way to be with him? But he had seemed as eager as she was to meet again, and he was certainly eager to make love to her—but not in the way she had visualised in her dreams.

She had tried to prevent him from drinking, but he had been too determined. This was something he had held in check during their short acquaintance before, and certainly, when he was in a normal frame of mind, he could be charming and good company. But the thrill had gone. She no longer loved him, and here she was in a strange country, thousands of miles from everything she knew, and what was more, she owed money for her fare to a man she had learned to dislike in less than two days. She was determined that she could not live under any obligation to Blake. She must find some way to pay him off and to save for her return fare. But that meant working for him, and working for him meant being with Dion. What was she to do?

At last, although she had thought she would never sleep, she must have dozed off, but she was suddenly awake, feeling stiff, tired and bewildered, not knowing for a few moments where she could be. Something had awakened her. Oh, yes, the whining sounds of a dog, scratching the door, eagerly trying to get in. There it came again, but this time there was the sound of a heavy body pushing against the door. It must be Honey, the golden spaniel. She must get up and stop him before he broke the glass panel. As she let him in, he circled around her barking with loud yelps.

'Oh, stop it, Honey,' she implored him. 'It's only me. I'm not doing any harm. Don't be ridiculous!'

She was not scared of the dog, only afraid he would awaken the whole household with his noise. He was wagging his short stump of a tail but still leaping around her making deep penetrating barks. Gemma knelt and seized him by the collar, hoping to calm him down, but still he persisted, though now he seemed glad to see her and covered her face with wet kisses. She was suddenly aware of the light from a large torch coming towards her from the direction of the house. Now what? she thought. She found herself wishing that the noise had aroused one of the servants and not, please not, Blake.

Her heart sank, however, as she recognised that voice, deep and challenging.

'Who's there? Come out, whoever you are!'

As she felt his eyes upon her, she wondered what she must look like, dishevelled as she was, her dress torn at the bodice showing too much of her breasts, her shoulders bare, her skirt also ripped.

'Gemma, what are you doing here?' His eyes narrowed. 'Have you been having some lovers' quarrel?'

'I suppose you could call it that,' Gemma told him. 'Have you any objection to my staying here? Honey seems to have.'

'Honey's a fool,' said Blake, his long fingers caressing the dog's silky ears. He had stopped his barking and was whining delightedly at Blake's feet. 'What is it, Gemma? Why have you come here?'

Gemma sought frantically for an answer. She could never tell him the truth, that she had ceased to love Dion and that he had nearly raped her.

'This is what you wanted, isn't it, that I should isolate myself from Dion the night before the race? Well, now you have your way! I'm sleeping here rather than spoil his chances as you said I might.'

'Seems rather a drastic measure,' he commented. 'I hope Dion appreciates it. Couldn't you just have locked yourself in, or merely said no? I thought girls were good at saying no sometimes.'

'This is my way of saying no,' said Gemma.

His glance encompassed her bare shoulders, the central hollow of her breasts.

'Or was it locking the stable door?' he asked.

'Certainly not! I care about Dion's safety as much as you do—more, in fact.'

'What do you mean by that?'

'I mean you needn't have tempted him back to motor racing, especially as you know he seems inclined to drink too much, a habit he didn't seem to have when I knew him before.'

'Oh, Dion's all right. I'm sure he kept sober in your company today, didn't he?'

Gemma felt disinclined to give Dion away. Blake would be furious if he knew how intoxicated Dion had become. She only hoped he could sleep it off by morning. She was startled to feel Blake's hand on her bare shoulder.

'Why are you shivering?' he asked. 'It gets cold at this time of night, some time before dawn. Why, girl, you feel frozen! Come inside and we'll concoct some kind of hot drink for you and I'll find you a jersey.'

'No, I'll be quite all right here, really, Blake.'

'Nonsense—come along. I feel partly responsible for your being here, though I hardly thought you would take my instructions quite so literally. However, it's just as well you did. Dion stands a much better chance of winning the race tomorrow if there's been no nonsense about making love to a girl beforehand.'

'And that's all you think about, isn't it, that he should win the race! You don't think that I've come thousands of miles to be with him, that I should be the most important thing in his life at this moment in time?'

Gemma was unnerved by the touch of his hand on her shoulder, by a feeling that she would have liked it to linger there. I'm in need of comfort, she thought, that's what it is, but not from this hateful man.

'So that's what's bugging you?' he said now. In the moonlight shining through the glass, his face had that mocking smile that she felt she had known for ever and not just for two days. 'You're jealous of the fact that Dion is taking part in this race. All your sights are set on that wedding dress and being the most important person at your little show, but, my dear Gemma, the race will be over tomorrow night and you'll have the rest of your life with Dion if you both wish it.'

I don't wish it now, she thought sadly, but she could not confess this to Blake.

'Come along, I'll find you a hot drink and a bed. There are always a few made up in the spare rooms.'

His arm was around her shoulder and she could not resist as he drew her over the patio and towards a side door into the house. Moonlight lay on the gleaming yellow-wood floor and darkened the blue of the Delft plates on the glossy carved dresser. The kitchen still had its old wide fireplace with the Dutch oven for bread and the spit for roasting joints, but there was more modern equipment too, and Blake proceeded to heat milk quite competently for one who seemed so very undomesticated. He poked at the fading coals of the hearth and the glow thus produced dispelled the last of Gemma's shivering.

'There's very little left of the night,' said Blake when they had finished the drink, 'but you'd better get some sleep. There's a long day behind and ahead of you too if you intend to go to see Dion race. Come along, I'll show you your room.'

Gemma did not want to disturb Dion now. She was uncertain how things would be when she went back to the cottage, so she followed Blake meekly up the stairs, hung on either side with family portraits, and accepted the room allotted to her, a room prettily papered with old sprigged silky paper. The small fourposter bed was hung with cream silk curtains and a Chinese carpet in pastel colours covered the floor.

'You can have some pyjamas if you wish, but as

you're a modern girl I presume you don't go in for nightwear,' said Blake.

She shook her head, for she did not want to trespass any more on Blake's reluctant hospitality by borrowing any garment he might produce. When he had gone, she took off the damaged sun-dress, feeling as if she never wanted to see it again, and slipped thankfully under the duvet that was covered with small sprays of pink, blue and yellow flowers.

Then she suddenly remembered the key. She had slipped it into the pocket of the dress when she had locked the door. If Dion woke before she did, as he might quite possibly do, he would not be able to get out of the cottage. He would recall the events of the night before and quite possibly be very ill-tempered, more especially if he found himself locked in. Somehow she must get out of the house again and go back to the cottage and unlock the door before he woke. But suppose he woke when she went back? Suppose the happenings of the night should be repeated? Dared she ask Blake to do this for her? She would tell him some story that would not give Dion away.

Having made up her mind to this, she drew a sheet around her, draped it in the fashion of a toga and went out into the passage. There was a light under one of the doors. This must be Blake's room, and she knocked lightly, clutching the sheet around her with the other hand. The door was flung open.

'What now?' asked Blake.

He was clad in a pair of briefs, his chest bare, the dark hairs in a V over the tanned pectoral muscles, his waist seeming very slim by the contrast with his broad shoulders. It was a shock to her to see him like this. If she had thought at all, she would have expected him to be in some rich robe, crimson brocade maybe, and now, seeing him half naked, the impact of him was strongly physical, and somehow magnetic in a way she had not dreamed of before. She found herself stumbling into speech.

'I'm sorry to disturb you like this. I forgot I had the key to the cottage, and when Dion wakes he won't be able to get out. Oh, Blake, could you possibly take it and unlock the door? I don't want to go back there yet.'

'Evidently not.'

His eyes were on her and she was conscious that the sheet had slipped, revealing her bare shoulders, and below it had come apart, making a background for her long slim legs.

Blake's head went back and his long brown torso quivered with laughter.

'So you locked him in! You were most obedient to my wishes, I must say, or was that how you wanted it to be?'

His laughter aroused her anger.

'It was only common sense, as you told me, to leave Dion to himself on the night of such an important race. It was what I thought should happen, even if Dion was a little reluctant to fall in with my wishes.'

'In other words, he didn't think much of it, and I can hardly blame him if you looked to him as you look to me right this minute. If Dion wasn't a good friend of mine, I might be tempted to ... oh, well, forget it. Where's the key?'

He had taken a step towards her when he said this and for a moment Gemma was breathlessly aware of him, so close to her that she could sense that elusive male fragrance that he seemed to carry about him, clean, cool as snow water, and yet deeply fascinating. She handed him the key, and as their fingers touched, with a quick movement he turned her around so that her back was towards him. For a moment he pressed her against him, his hands at her waist, and then so swiftly that she thought she had imagined the hardness of that male body so close to hers, he released her and, giving her a slight push, commanded, 'Go and get some sleep. I'll see to unlocking that door.'

But it was a long time before she slept.

When she awoke, it was still quite early. Doves murmured sleepily from the oaks and a large bird burnished brown and white gave a liquid call like bubbling spring water right near to her window. Her sleep had been troubled by dreams, but she could not remember them now, yet she was still disturbed by a sense of hidden menace and she felt somehow threatened. By Dion? The golden sunlight made nonsense of her dreams. She must go to him now, make friends with him again. Last night had been like a bad dream, nothing more. He would repent his behaviour when sober. If she was to work here, and it seemed as if she would have to, she could not afford to have Dion hostile and unhappy. It was up to her to find the man she had known and thought she had loved two years ago. They must find each other again.

Any man might have behaved like Dion had done when he had had too much to drink. Why, even Blake.... She remembered with astonishment her own reaction when he had looked at her with those gold-green eyes and shown quite plainly that he considered her desirable if she had not, as he thought, belonged to Dion. If she could feel that tremble of delight at the thought of Blake's touch when she did not even like him and he was practically a stranger, how could she blame Dion for getting carried away when they had been apart for all these months?

She arose and showered quickly in the pale green and white bathroom that was part of her suite, casting a rather envious glance at the shining new fittings, the flowered tiles, and the soft apple green bath sheets. Then reluctantly putting on her sun-dress, that by now looked rather the worse for wear, she slipped quietly down the stairs. A young servant was sweeping the patio and bade her good morning with a singular lack of curiosity, and a tempting fragrance of coffee came from the direction of the kitchen, but otherwise there was no sign of life, and she breathed a sigh of relief. She would have hated to face Blake just yet.

All was still at the cottage as she slipped quietly into the unlocked door. The key was on the inside, so Blake must have made good his promise, and Dion was still asleep, stretched out on his bed, clothed as he had been yesterday. There was a blanket over his feet. Had Blake put it there, and, if so, how much had he suspected? Would he realise that Dion had had too much to drink yesterday? Gemma changed into neat white slacks and a blue striped shirt, and while she was boiling the kettle for coffee, she heard Dion stirring in the other room. Would he be furious with her? If so, she decided it could not be helped. She felt better able to deal with him now that daylight had come and she had had some rest. He strolled into the kitchen yawning and running his fingers through his long hair. His eyes were a little bloodshot, but otherwise he looked normal.

'Hi, Gemma, you're a sight for sore eyes, and mine are sore literally! I have a feeling I drank a little too much wine yesterday. Did we enjoy ourselves last night? I hope so. I intended to show you a good time, but unfortunately I can't remember a thing. I only know I had a very good few hours' sleep. I hope you did too.'

'Yes, Dion, we had a super day and a gorgeous dinner. I hope it hasn't left you too tired for the race.'

'Not a bit of it. I feel great. Only I can't remember a thing that happened after we had dinner. Tell me, Gemma, did I make love to you? That's what I intended.'

'No, Dion, you didn't. You fell asleep.'

'Did I really? What a sad waste of opportunity! Sorry about that. Better luck next time. We'll celebrate my victory tonight, I hope.'

So he didn't remember anything of last night's happenings. Would he not have remembered even if he had made love to her? Gemma wondered. She felt relieved and yet uneasy, for how could she deal with him on future occasions? She would have to make herself clear some time, but not this morning; she did not want to upset him before the big race. She made coffee and he seemed content to caress her mildly, and although after last night she found even this difficult to tolerate, she tried not to notice it too much, as she realised his mind was not on her but upon the coming events of the day. She noticed his hand shook slightly as she handed him the mug of coffee.

'Dion, are you sure you're all right for today?'

He glanced up sharply.

'Your hand's shaking,' Gemma pointed out.

'Nonsense, I'm as steady as a rock. Anyhow, this coffee is putting me right. I had a headache when I woke, but I know what will cure that.'

He opened a cupboard and took out a bottle of some brown liquid. Sloshing it into his mug together with the coffee, he drained the mixture off before Gemma had time to realise what he was about.

'Dion, what was that?' she asked anxiously.

'Brandy, my dear girl, aqua vitae, elixir of life, guaranteed to cure a hangover with a hair of the dog, only it's not quite the same hair. This is export quality, specially saved for an occasion like this, when I really need it.'

'But you don't need it, Dion. You just said you feel fine.'

'I'll feel finer now I've had this little *soopie*. It's going to do me a whole lot of good, you'll see. I'm going to take some with me too, to give me a bit of get up and go for the big race.'

'Don't drink any more, Dion, please,' Gemma pleaded. She was appalled that he had drunk this brandy, for Blake had especially warned her not to let him have any spirits.

'Don't worry, my love, it was only a very little. You are a darling to be so concerned about me, aren't you? You really do love me, don't you, Gemma? Aren't I the lucky one? I've got an interesting job, a super car to drive and a beautiful girl who's going to watch me win the race, and afterwards she's going to let me make love to her as she's never been made love to before. That's so, isn't it?'

He didn't wait for an answer but swung Gemma off her feet and was just about to kiss her when there was a discreet cough at the door. Shadrac stood there, a tray in his hand, the plates covered with silver domes.

'Master said I should bring breakfast here. He thought you would like to have it alone with the young madame. There's some grilled steak and eggs and coffee. He says you must make a good breakfast.'

'Sounds like I'm a condemned criminal,' said Dion, but he smiled and released Gemma from the grip around her waist. 'Come on, let's eat! Perhaps you were right—that brandy has made me just a trifle woozy. Nothing that a good steak and some coffee won't cure!'

CHAPTER FOUR

BLAKE took them to the race track in his silver Mercedes, and, driving along in the sunshine with the blue mountains towering in the background, Gemma was relieved to think that Dion seemed none the worse for his over-indulgence last night and his early drink this morning. He was excited certainly, talking rather loudly to Blake, who sat at the wheel making the occasional comment. How different were the backs of the two men's heads, Gemma thought, Dion's with the luxuriant blond locks, Blake's dark, gleaming and closely cropped. She herself sat in the rear of the huge car and both men seemed completely unaware that she was there, so absorbed were they in talk about the coming race.

'Try to remember the things I told you, Dion. Don't let the wheel spin, keep your hands on it. You must be able to unwind the wheel if you get into a jam. If you get into a skid, turn the wheel towards it and don't brake too early when you get to a corner.'

'Good grief, Blake, don't you think I know all that?'

'Of course you do, but in the excitement of the race you're apt to forget. A bit of a reminder won't do you any harm.'

Dion turned towards Blake and Gemma could see that the set of his mouth was sullen.

'You aren't the only racing driver in the world, Blake. Give me credit for knowing a little about it too!'

'Sorry, old chap, it's just that I know the car so well and I'm apt to think no one else understands her as I do. I'm sure you'll do splendidly, but it's just these little extra points that make the difference between winning and being one of the crowd.'

It wasn't like Blake to apologise, thought Gemma. He must be particularly anxious that Dion should win. And was Dion really fit after last night? Ought she to tell Blake of her doubts? But Dion seemed perfectly all right now and they would both be furious if she tried to interfere. If she could see Blake alone, should she say anything? But if he was satisfied that Dion was competent, what would be the point? It would only be salving her own conscience and lead to trouble between the two men if she mentioned that Dion had had too much to drink yesterday. And that was yesterday, anyway. Today he seemed fit enough and as he had said he was used to drinking wine. She hardly thought it would impair his judgment today.

Arriving at the race track, she felt overwhelmed by the heat and noise of the crowd. There was such a hectic atmosphere, enough to make her nerves tauten like the strings on a violin. In the clear sunlit air, the sound of racing cars being tuned sounded like an enormous hive of killer bees, and the shouting of instructions through the loudhailer was larger than life and seemed more than human ears could stand. When they had made their way to the pits, the mechanics were putting last touches to a silver and blue racing car.

'Here she is,' said Dion. 'Isn't she a beauty?'

To Gemma, it did not look like a car at all, more like some monstrous insect in a science fiction film, streamlined and geared to kill. What nonsense, she chided herself. It's only a heap of metal, though you would never think so, the way these men are hovering over it as if it were the most beautiful object ever created. And there were girls there too, glamorous beauties in brief shorts with long brown legs, bare golden shoulders and tiny tops, tossing their long blonde hair as they talked to Dion and Blake. Gemma felt sedate and old compared with these teenagers. With her white slacks and blue and white striped shirt, she had dressed in a practical manner because she knew the day in the open might play havoc with her pale English skin. Already after yesterday, her neck and shoulders were somewhat pink, but these girls must spend their days on the beach, by the looks of it. Their skins were golden and beautiful and they looked utterly glamorous as they clustered around Blake and Dion, in the meantime carefully keeping an eye on the news photographers and T.V. men to try to get into the picture.

'That's it, then,' she heard Blake say. 'Come along, Gemma, we'd better get out of the way.'

The young girls reluctantly drifted away and she saw that Dion was about to put on his heavy headgear, that made him look like something from outer space. Before he could do so, she had a sudden impulse to embrace him, a feeling of sadness that nothing had turned out as it should have done.

'Goodbye, Dion,' she murmured. 'Take care of yourself, and do well.'

She lifted her face up and they kissed. It was slow and tender, this embrace. This is how it should have been before, she thought. This is how it can be again.

'Come along, Gemma,' she heard Blake say impatiently. 'We must get to our seats. No time to lose.'

'Tonight,' she heard Dion say. 'Tonight, Gemma, I'll show you how to love.'

She knew that Blake must have heard. He was standing so close, he could not have failed to hear it, but his face expressed neither approval nor otherwise. He clapped Dion on the shoulder.

'Don't think of anything else but the race, old man,' he advised.

He means don't think of me, thought Gemma. So he does disapprove. He thinks Dion should have made me put off my arrival until the race was over, but it was I who was so eager to come, and now I think I wish I hadn't.

There were seats for them on the open stand opposite the starting grid where gradually the racing cars were assembling. Opposite was the long line of pits, and Gemma could see that the mechanics were still fussing around with the blue and silver car.

'Blake, why aren't you in the race, man?'

Some people behind them greeted Blake, and his attention was diverted from the scene in front of them. Gemma, still watching Dion, saw him take off his heavy helmet and lift a silver flask to his lips. Oh, no, she thought. He must have brought some spirits with him after all. Should she tell Blake? But it was too late now. The heavy vehicles were making their way slowly to their positions on the starting line and the marshals stood with flags at the ready. And then they were off and away, racing down the straight like eager greyhounds.

'He's got a good start,' said Blake, as Dion extricated himself from the crowd of cars and forged ahead. The announcements blasted away from the loudspeakers, giving the progress of the competitors.

'Have you ever watched a race before?' Blake asked Gemma.

'Never,' Gemma answered. 'It's never been my scene.'

'Well, you have something to look forward to now, then. You'll have plenty of thrills in the future, because Dion and I are pretty determined to make it our scene. So it will have to be yours as well, won't it?'

'I guess so,' said Gemma. Already she was hating the heat, the noise, the smell of fuel. 'I don't know that I can get very excited about it, but maybe I can try,' she added.

'It's a thrilling pastime. If you knew how frustrated I feel not being able to go in it today you'd be surprised!'

Nothing about you could surprise me, thought Gemma.

She was very conscious of his nearness, pressed up against him by the crowded seats, his thigh warm against her own, their shoulders touching. What was it about him that made him so disturbing in spite of the fact that he obviously disapproved of her?

The streamlined cars thundered around the circuit like so many toys upon a mechanised rail and the noise of them beat into her brain until there seemed to be nothing else in the world except the screaming sound of exhausts and revving engines. All around them people yelled in delight as their particular favourites came into sight. Every now and again the radio system crackled and a loud, excited voice would announce that this or that driver was out of the race, but Dion drove on. At each lap they saw the huge silver and blue monster hurtling around.

But on the sixth lap, Blake exclaimed, 'Oh, lord, he's swaying! There seems to be something wrong with a tyre!'

They saw him draw up at the pits and the mechanics hastened to change a wheel. As they did so, Gemma again saw him remove his headgear and take a swig at the silver flask, but this time Blake had seen it too.

'The fool! he muttered. 'I told him not to carry liquor on him. Did you know he had it?'

Gemma stuttered some reply. She had not known until she saw him just before the race, but now she thought she should perhaps have said something to Blake. Blake was looking keenly at her now and, under the gaze of those dark direct eyes, she felt herself flushing uncomfortably.

'I thought I warned you to keep him off drink. Well, I hope he hasn't spoiled his race by this stupidity. Naturally his reactions slow down when he's had alcohol and yet he takes more chances. Well, he's away now. I only hope it doesn't affect his judgment.'

And so do I, thought Gemma. She watched the cars hurtling around the bend towards them. More of them seemed to have retired. I wish Dion would withdraw too, she thought, but the blue and silver car kept coming up, faster and faster as the other ones dropped behind. He seemed to be going at the speed of light now, she thought, but the car was not firm on the road. It swayed from side to side as it hit the bend.

'He's overtaxing it,' said Blake, 'but he seems to be holding it well.'

Dion was way out ahead of the other cars, but now he was catching up on the slower cars that were on different laps, and seemed to be having difficulty avoiding them, yet nothing it seemed could make him slow down. The crowd shouted in mingled excitement and terror as he took daring chances, swaying around anything that came in his path.

'That assistant of yours sure can put the pressure on!' she heard the man behind her shout to Blake.

'He's taking too many chances,' answered Blake.

'He's over-confident.'

'Well, he seems to be on a winning streak.'

'I hope you're right.'

In the burning heat of the sun, Gemma sat petrified as if she had been turned to stone. She didn't know much about motor racing, but she could tell from Blake's expression that he was appalled at the way Dion was driving.

'He's not experienced enough to be taking all those risks,' he muttered.

'But if he's not experienced enough why did you put him in it at all?' asked Gemma.

It was dreadful to see Dion hurtling around the track swaying dangerously, putting other cars at risk, and not be able to stop him. Now all had become quiet. It seemed as if the huge crowd held its breath, for the shouts of excitement and encouragement had ceased, only the drumming noise of the engines beat their rapid tattoo into Gemma's ears. The car disappeared again around the bend and she was aware that Blake had put his hand over hers and was holding it firmly and reassuringly.

'Stop worrying, Gemma. It's almost over. He's on the last lap now and he's doing extraordinarily well in spite of his recklessness. Only another few minutes and he'll be wearing that victory garland and opening the champagne.'

'I wish it was all over,' said Gemma.

'He's almost there,' Blake told her.

And he was. There was just one bend to make before the finish. He was out of sight now and Gemma with the rest of the crowd waited for him to appear, but, as he reached this last corner, he seemed at last to lose control.

'Too fast!' she heard Blake shout. 'God save him, he's taken the corner too fast!'

It was like something on a film. It could not be actually happening. She saw the car drift outwards and cut the edge of the grass on the outer side of the kerb, the wheels spinning madly, and it came back on to the track, then off the track again on the other side.

'Oh, God, he's overcorrected!' muttered Blake.

She saw the car spin around like a top, round and around, with Dion a tiny figure at the wheel frantically seeming to unwind it, then the car flipped sideways, over and over, rolling like some drunken elephant, spewing out dust and pieces of metal with a noise that Gemma thought would be for ever in her brain, and then everything was still. It seemed as if the whole world stopped for a matter of seconds, and yet to Gemma it seemed like years before people started running to the place at the finishing line where the broken car lay on its back, its wheels still feebly spinning.

Other cars flashed by and the marshals' flags were down, and yet the crowd didn't even cheer. Everything was concentrated on the ruined vehicle and the efforts of the mechanics to raise it.

'Don't look,' said Blake. 'I must go down there. Will you be all right?'

Gemma nodded blindly. I'll never be all right again, she thought.

'Will you let me know at once if. . . .' she whispered.

Blake nodded and turned to the man who had spoken to him previously.

'Miles, will you stay with Gemma? Perhaps you should take her back to the farm. It would be better to get her right away—I'm likely to be delayed.'

Miles looked at her pityingly, holding her arm, supporting her, and she realised that Blake was making his way down to the track, where people were milling around the shattered car.

'Blake said you'd come from England only the other day,' Miles said. 'Was Dion your boy-friend?'

When Gemma heard him use the past tense, she knew what she had tried not to believe. The crowd knew too. It was passing from lip to lip the fact that Dion was dead.

'You look very pale. Would you like some brandy?'

He produced a silver flask, almost identical to the one she had seen Dion use. She gave a choking laugh.

'Oh, no, I couldn't. I'd be sick. I never want to see or smell brandy again.'

She tried not to look at the scene below, and she tried to quell the waves of blackness that kept rising up to meet her. She felt sorry for the man who had been left in charge of her. He looked so helpless.

'Don't worry about me. I'll be all right,' she told him. 'But I must get away. I just want to go home.'

Home? she thought. Where's that? Not now the cottage that she had thought would be so pretty once she and Dion were married. Not, certainly not, the big beautiful house with its graceful gables.

'I'll take you back. Obviously Blake will have to stay here for a while.'

Her mind felt blank as the stranger drove her back to the farm. He kept glancing sideways at her and she tried to speak to him, but it all seemed too much effort, for what could she say? Blake must have phoned home the news to Shadrac, because he was waiting with coffee in a silver pot set out on a tray with fine china cups. Again Gemma refused to have anything stronger, but sipped a black coffee gratefully while the stranger drank whisky.

'I feel as if I need this,' said Miles. 'Are you sure you won't have any? It would do you good.'

'No, the coffee's all I need. I'm sorry you've had all this trouble, bringing me home and so on. I'm afraid I'm poor company. I can't seem to think of anything to say.'

Miles looked at her pityingly.

'Good Lord, don't apologise! It's terrible for you. I'm sorry there isn't anything I can do to help you. I guess Blake will be home soon, and you'll be able to talk to him.'

She could not tell him that she had begun to dread meeting Blake again. She still could not think straight, and yet she knew behind all her stunned silence that hovering there was a dreadful feeling of guilt, a desperate sense that somehow she could have prevented Dion's death.

Left alone at last, she made her way back to the cottage. She must face it some time, but when she got there it seemed too much to bear. Dion's bed was still rumpled from his sleep, the coffee cups still on the table. Gemma went quickly into her room and shut the door. Then she lay with her face to the wall, her eyes tracing the tiny tracks in the faded distemper, but like a T.V. screen before her she saw the track and the ruined car, and although outside the sun was still hot, and although she pulled the blankets around her chin, she was seized with a violent trembling that she could not control. She did not hear the footsteps crossing the living room and, when she heard the light knock on the door, she felt incapable of answering. The door opened, but still she lay there, shivering and cold, her eyes closed to the light, as if she could blot out the pictures in her mind.

'Gemma,' she heard Blake's voice, but still she could not respond to him. He strode across to her and she felt his hands supporting her, raising her into a sitting position.

'Don't. I can't. . . .' she whispered brokenly.

'My poor girl, you can't stay alone like this. I've sent Shadrac to the doctor's surgery to get something you can take to calm your nerves, something to make you sleep.'

'I don't need anything. I don't feel as if I'll ever sleep again.'

'Look, if it's any help I can tell you that Dion died instantly. He couldn't have known anything about it after the first seconds.'

'But oh, why did it have to happen like that?' she wailed. 'He was so happy yesterday, and this morning he was looking forward to so much.'

'Yes, I know,' said Blake.

Was he remembering Dion's last words to her? Tonight I'll show you how to love. Now she recalled the night before with bitter regret. Why had everything gone wrong? Why couldn't she have felt the tenderness she had felt from him when he gave her that last kiss? If she had known . . . but that was stupid. And yet she felt a terrible guilt that she had refused him last night, that she had fled away from him when he wanted to make love to her. If he had been happy with her maybe he would not have needed to drink during the race. Was it all her fault? Hers and Blake's, for Blake in spite of his doubts about Dion had urged him to go into the race.

'There's Shadrac,' said Blake now. 'You must take one of the tablets he's brought. I'll get you some water.'

When he had come from the kitchen with a glass of water, she swallowed the tablet down. She felt too weak to argue. He looked around the room as if it were the first time he had seen it properly.

'This whole place looks very shabby. I'm surprised, because I thought Dion had ideas for redecorating it. I gave him the materials to get it done.'

'It hardly matters now, does it?' said Gemma.

She felt ashamed that she had criticised Dion in her own mind for not making more effort to prepare the cottage for her coming.

'I'll get it done,' said Blake. 'You'll need more convenient living quarters if you're going to work here.'

She looked at him, wide-eyed.

'But I can't stay here now!'

'Of course you can. There's a job waiting for you here. What else do you propose to do?'

'I don't know. I have to think.'

'Don't worry about it now. Just try to sleep.' He tucked the blankets around her once more and drew the curtains. 'You should sleep for a while and later I'll send Shadrac with a light supper.'

'I couldn't eat anything,' Gemma whispered.

'You should try. Anyhow, I'll send it and come to see you later.'

When he had gone, she thought, what's to happen to me now? I'm bound to work here for Blake because he paid my fare, and there's that contract too. If only I could pay it back. But where can I go if I don't work here? I can't possibly buy my fare back to England, and I wouldn't like to borrow it from Blake because I already owe him for the other ticket. Oh, Dion, why am I thinking of myself? If I hadn't been so careful of myself, so ungenerous, you might still be here. She was seized up in a paroxysm of grief for him and everything that had gone wrong, and, even when the drug took effect, over and over again she jerked awake, seeing before her the nightmare scene of the crash, but presently she drifted into a deeper sleep and for a little while forgot the tragedy of this day.

CHAPTER FIVE

'WE both need to get away. I can leave Shadrac in charge over a weekend—at this time of year everything is running smoothly. What do you say to flying to the Wild Coast? I can borrow a small chalet from a friend and we'll have two days away from all this.'

'But I couldn't go away with you,' protested Gemma. 'In the first place, I can't afford the flight ticket.'

The awful week had passed and the numbness she had felt at Dion's death had gone. In its place was a great sadness that she had been with him for so short a time and that she had not felt the love she had thought they had for each other. Now it was as if they were still apart as they had been before, but now there was nothing to look forward to, and she must try to cope with the strangeness of this new life on her own.

'Why couldn't you go away with me?' queried Blake. 'I assure you I have no designs on your virtue.'

'I didn't think you had, and it's kind of you to think of taking me away, but as I said before, I really can't afford it.'

'But I can. Look, Gemma, I really think you deserve a break before you start working. Have this one on me. You'll enjoy the Wild Coast and you'll come back refreshed and feeling a new woman.'

'That would be great. I don't much like the woman I am at the moment,' she admitted.

I don't like the feeling of guilt, she thought, the idea that I could have done more to stop Dion's dizzy path towards death. She did not want to be more involved with Blake than she was; she was enough in his debt already.

'Won't people think it odd if we go away together so soon after Dion's death?' she asked now.

'What people? No one's going to worry about it one way or the other. Look, girl, I'm proposing this for your own good. You don't think I intend to seduce you, do you?'

'No.'

You don't even like me, she thought. You're only doing your best to be kind because of Dion. Perhaps if I go away, somewhere else, somewhere where every step I take doesn't remind me of Dion, I'll stop having these dreams about the crash and I can think things out, decide what's the best thing to do, not drift along in this aimless way that I'm doing now.

'All right, I'll come with you,' she told him.

'Fine! I'll book straight away. All you'll need there is slacks and shorts, a couple of shirts and a swimsuit. We'll pick up some provisions on the way, but there's a small hotel there where we could get a meal. We'll take fishing rods—there's nothing like a spot of fishing, sitting on the rocks, watching the waves break, to clear the brain.'

It was not until Gemma was sitting in the plane and the sea below was washing in creamy scallops towards the coastline that she thought to herself, what am I doing here? I must be mad! Here I am going away for the weekend with a man who is a stranger, and who is only being kind to me because he feels obliged to be on account of Dion's death. And I'm going to this place at his expense, I, who have always tried to be independent, who wouldn't even borrow money from my sister, when she offered to lend me the fare to get here, before Dion sent the ticket.

Blake sat beside her saying very little, just occasionally pointing out places of interest far down below. In spite of her doubts, she could not help being enthralled by the panorama unfolding itself far beneath her. It was a glorious day, sunlit and vividly blue, and the coastline was clear with a deeper blue ocean flecked by white waves with every now and again stretches of golden sand. On the land side there was a thick band of trees and mountains looking like a relief map.

'The Tsitsikama Forest stretches for a long way. It's natural woodland, and behind it are the Outeniqua mountains,' Blake informed her. 'And on the other side of the mountains is the long Kloof where you get a climate very suitable for fruit growing. That's where most of the apples are grown.'

Gemma tried to take an intelligent interest in what he was saying, to overcome the numbness and grief that had afflicted her since that dreadful day. The awful thing was that she found now she could hardly remember how Dion had looked in the two days she had known him here. He had seemed so different. What she remembered and wanted to remember was the Dion who had attracted her in Spain when they had first met. When she tried to think of him as he had been, in reality, a fog seemed to rise up in her mind.

Especially she tried to forget that last night, and how she had refused him when he had wanted to make love to her. Now she thought of herself as ungenerous, wondering whether she should have surrendered to his wishes. Would she have done so if she had known this was to be his last night on earth? In her grief she had forgotten the ugly part of it, how rough, how demanding, how untender he had been. She only thought that she had largely been to blame for his drinking more than he should have so that it affected his judgment in the race.

And she blamed herself for not loving him, because that was why she had refused him, because she was no longer attracted to him as she had been before. I wish I'd never come here, she thought. But if she had never come here, she would never have known that love had gone. It seemed a bitter irony now, that even though she had not even known about the suggestion that she should work for Blake, here she was now, tied to a man she had disliked as soon as she met him, unable to get away because she was still in his debt.

And I'm even more in his debt now, she thought, glancing sideways. Blake had closed his eyes and like this somehow looked younger and more vulnerable, the harsh expression of the lips softened in sleep. There was something intimate about this journey, sitting close together, high above Africa, the large seats hiding the other passengers from view. His hand slipped sideways and touched hers and she didn't take it away, even when as if accidentally it covered her own. There was something comforting about the warmth of his body close to hers and she let it rest there, even though she felt he might be dreaming of someone else as his hand now slid along her bare arm.

The announcement that they were descending to East London, the coast town in the Eastern Province, aroused him, and he sat up, fastening his seatbelt and straightening the seat.

'Did I drop off? I've not been sleeping too well,' he told her.

Me neither, thought Gemma.

'We take a smaller plane to reach the Wild Coast,' he said now. 'It's a perfect day and shouldn't be too bumpy.'

And soon they were flying along a rugged coastline with natural forest in a dark green fringe right down to the shining sea, and rolling green country dotted with round African huts on the hillsides. They were flying so low that they could see the outlines of the cattle kraals with aloes in clumps around them, and the herds of cows upon the green grass undisturbed as the shadow of the plane passed over them.

'Hi there, do you need a lift?'

As they descended on to the airstrip, a man, sunburned and in khaki shorts and safari jacket, approached them from the jeep that was standing nearby.

'We'd be glad of it,' said Blake.

'I was expecting some guests for the hotel, but they haven't arrived yet. You'll be the ones for Dolphin Cottage, I take it. I was told you were coming and we got in the provisions you ordered.'

'Good,' said Blake. 'We'll probably eat at the hotel in the evenings—that is, if we don't catch fish.'

'Oh, you'll do that all right. The grunter are still running in the river mouth. There've been some good catches lately.'

The jeep bounced along a rough path, swinging around curves, and deposited them in front of a cottage that was standing on its own, isolated from the few buildings that were around. As Gemma descended from the vehicle, she smelled the herblike fragrance of the rough vegetation and the sharp tang of the sea. It was a long, low cottage, painted white, with a straight room in the middle and two rooms, curved and thatched like the African huts, on either end. The cottage was a little way above the beach, and below them was the whole sweep of yellow sand and blue sea with banana palms and wild bush edging the circular bay.

'It looks like Paradise,' Gemma said. And yet as she saw the jeep drawing away and was left alone with Blake, she had to quell a feeling of dismay. She had not known what to expect, but here she was in almost absolute isolation with a man she hardly knew and did not know whether she could trust.

Blake had got the key from the man in the jeep, and now he unlocked the door and ushered Gemma into a room that was neat and clean but not luxurious. There were a small table and chairs, an old but comfortable settee and an old yellow-wood dresser with coloured plates and some large shells upon it. Fishing rods leaned in one corner, together with surfboards. In the round room where Gemma was to sleep, she found a narrow bed with a flat hard mattress, a deal cupboard and a few unpainted shelves, a china wash basin and jug on an old-fashioned stand and a large tin bath on one side of the room.

'Here you mostly depend upon the sea for washing,' Blake told her. 'Fortunately it's almost always warm. We can manage without the amenities just for a weekend, don't you agree?'

'Yes, certainly,' said Gemma.

In fact she was rather relieved. If she had found that Blake had brought her to some luxurious place, she might have suspected that this was a cottage to which he customarily brought his girl-friends, but this was so basic that you could hardly call it a love-nest. No, he had just wanted to get away, as he had said, and thought it would do her good too to have a change. It was more the kind of place where men would come for a weekend's fishing. He had just brought her because he was trying to cheer her after this awful week.

'So how about a bathe while the weather's good and the tide's right? There'll be plenty of time for fishing later,' Blake told her. She had bought this bikini with a honeymoon in mind, bright sunshine yellow decorated with dark blue seahorses. It showed more of her body than she would have chosen to display to Blake, but that couldn't be helped. Although she pulled in vain at the tiny bra with its thin halter straps, the curves of her slight breasts remained obstinately uncovered. Oh, heavens, she had hoped Dion would find her alluring in this two-piece garment that showed off her slim body, the long slim legs, the lissom curving waist, but now she felt embarrassed at showing off her body to Blake. Don't be stupid, she told herself, you're not the first girl he's seen in a scanty costume.

He hardly seemed to look at her as she joined him and walked down to the beach. He too was in a brief swimsuit, his whole body a uniform shade of bronze, the powerful shoulders a striking contrast to the slim hips and long strong legs.

'What kind of a swimmer are you?' he asked her.

'Quite good, I think. I used to win events at school.'

He grinned as if she had said something funny.

'The Indian Ocean isn't exactly like the school swimming bath, you know! Don't venture out too far the first time. You'll find the breakers a bit much at first. Dive under them if you feel they're going to knock you down, but it's more fun to ride them. I'll show you how.'

As they entered the water and it became deeper around them, the waves splashed deliciously around her body that had been heated by the journey and the rough ride in the torrid sun of the afternoon. In front of her the breakers seemed like shivering green hills in perpetual motion, rolling towards the shore to reach a peak and crash in a shining welter of white foam a few yards from the edge. Blake took her hand, as she swayed to the motion of the sea.

'Dive under this one!' he shouted above the noise of the breakers, and, trying to follow him, Gemma let herself glide into the emerald heart of the wave, emerging on the other side as it crashed with a noise like thunder upon the beach.

'Well done, now try riding with the wave,' she heard him say. His arm was around her and she was conscious of his touch, wet on her bare shoulders. 'Watch the wave. When it arrives here but before it breaks, put your arms out and go with it just before the peak,' he told her.

Holding her, he guided her arms and said, 'Now!' She felt herself carried along just ahead of the breaking line of foam. It carried her shorewards, with Blake beside her in an exhilarating ride.

'That was wonderful,' she said. 'I felt like a dolphin, or perhaps a mermaid.'

Now, for the first time in days, she was able to forget the thing that had figured so tragically in her mind since the day of the race. She forgot everything but the sensation of coasting upon the surging water with Blake beside her, guiding her, keeping her safe. Her hair hung in damp streamers around her face and her blue eyes stung with the tang of salt, but she felt as if she were in her natural element and that she could go on like this for ever as if she were really a mermaid. There was a kind of ecstasy in surrendering so completely to something stronger than oneself.

'It's simply glorious! I've never known anything like it,' she gasped as, quite without hesitation, she clung to Blake and he held her to prevent the waves from sweeping her away. His eyes within inches of her own, she noticed now, were the golden brown of peat water and fringed with long lashes, wet, spiky, black. She looked at the dark pelt of wet curls upon his chest and was suddenly conscious of his hands upon her own naked body. Memory swept over her. How could she be enjoying this deeply physical pleasure when Dion was in his grave?

'All the same, I think I'll go in now. I've had enough for one day.'

'Fair enough. Go and catch the late sun. I'll bathe a little more—I won't be long.'

Back on the beach, Gemma dried herself and lay on the towel, facing towards the waves, her chin on her hands, feeling the hot sun on her back. Blake had gone farther out now. She watched rather anxiously as his dark head appeared like a seal far out to sea, much farther than she would have thought was safe. But he knows what he's doing, she assured herself, because he's used to this life. All the same, she began to wish she had stayed with him. He would have remained in the shallows then, helping her. But then wasn't that rather boring for him? She must keep reminding herself that he was only being kind to her because of Dion, that normally he would have taken no notice of her at all. She was not his kind of girl, if the blonde one he had escorted at the party was anything to go by.

She strained to watch him now, the black seal's head far out in the waves and swimming fast arm over arm in front of the wet emerald mountains of the breakers. Tragedy makes you imagine tragedy, she thought. If he were to drown? Don't be stupid, Gemma. You're just in a highly nervous state—but oh, I do wish he would come out! She was relieved when she saw him walking towards her through the shallows, his shadow long before the afternoon sun, and he flung himself down beside her, water falling in iridescent rainbow drops from his shoulders.

'That was good. I feel as if I've been made over again. What about you?'

'Yes, it was wonderful. It's so different from the cold, flat English sea.'

'You can say that again! But you still have your pale English skin. We must try to do something about that, but you'll have to be careful. However, it's late afternoon now. You should be safe enough from excessive sunburn.'

'I thought I'd become a little suntanned,' she told him.

'Not so you'd notice.'

Gemma had a swift memory of the young girls who

had hung around Dion and Blake, young girls with golden peach-bloom skins on every inch of them. Of course to Blake she must look very pallid and insipid when he was used to girls like that. She was conscious of his eyes upon her now.

'When you've lived here for six months, you'll notice the difference. That ivory skin that goes with your kind of reddish gold hair often tans to a delightful shade.'

'How do you know I intend to stay here for six months?' she queried.

'Oh, I expect you will. I usually get what I set out to have, and I want you to start running the catering side of the farm to make a huge success of it.'

'That's still all you think of, isn't it?'

'It's an important part of my life, but it's not quite all I think of, not by any means.'

Gemma felt a shiver of doubt. There seemed to be some dark meaning in his expression as his glance swept over her unclothed body. She must be imagining it. Even now he seemed to think of her just as a useful person to employ and carry out his ideas. He did not seem to realise that for her life here must be blank without the incentive of marriage to Dion she had had before she came. Could she possibly stay here and work for Blake? There seemed to be no alternative now.

The shadows of the sandhills were long upon the beach and at last a cool breeze came in from the sea.

'Too late for fishing,' said Blake. 'We'll try tomorrow morning. We'll dine at the hotel tonight—much less trouble.'

I'll be even more in his debt if he isn't even going to rely on me to cook meals, Gemma thought.

She stood in the tin bath and sluiced water over her sandy sunburned limbs. In the little thatched room, still warm from the day's sun, it was deliciously cool to stand there and sponge her body with the soft spring water. Abbreviated underwear, sandals and a sun-dress were all she would need for dinner in the small hotel. By the glowing light of the oil lamp, she applied a little make-up, gazing rather anxiously at herself in the mirror that was old and tarnished by the sea air. Her hair was still damp and she piled it up into a knot on top of her head, letting the loose strands curl down on each side of her face. The pale green sprigged dress emphasised the copper-gold tints of her hair, and at last she seemed to be acquiring a bit of a tan, the ivory of her shoulders changed to a faint colour of creamy gold, her long legs a deeper shade of brown, like very delicate silk stockings.

When she emerged from the room, Blake had found a couple of chairs for the patio and had placed them there facing the sea.

'We'll have a glass of wine and watch the sun go down,' he decided.

He had changed into casual corded light khaki jeans and a zip-fronted jacket in a kind of deep cream velour. It emphasised the deep brown of his skin and the darkness of his hair. Gemma realised with something of a shock that he could look tremendously handsome. She had hardly thought about it before, so deeply had she been involved in thinking about Dion. He was evidently looking at her with new eyes too, because he swung her around and eyed her coiffure.

'The first time I've seen you with your hair up, and yet it seems to make you look younger rather than more sophisticated, as one would suppose.'

'I wasn't trying to look sophisticated. It was just the easiest way to deal with it because it was damp,' she explained.

She didn't want Blake to think she had altered her appearance in any way to be more attractive for him.

'Come, try this light sparkling wine—just the right wine for the view.'

'I don't really want to drink wine.'

'Come now, this is very light. I chose it specially for you because I know you aren't used to wine.'

Gemma started to sip it rather unhappily because it reminded her of that last day with Dion. If only she had been firmer about it then, she thought. But the beauty of the scene in front of her took her mind from her sadness. The sea was transformed now, grey silk taffeta shot with rose and gold, and above it a sky full of streamers of flame. One silver star shimmered in the darker blue, a forerunner of all the myriad that soon would appear in the African night.

'It's heavenly,' she said as if to herself, but Blake had heard her.

'I rather thought you'd like it,' he said, as if he had invented the scene himself.

The swift African twilight was giving place to night as they walked along the narrow track to the hotel, and Blake had brought a strong torch to light the way, but he held her arm too, because in the darkness the path was pitted and rough. Gemma felt very alone now. It was not the high season and there was little sign of life in the other cottages. Overhead the stars were appearing, though the western sky was still flushed with crimson and in the bush beside the sea there were numerous insect noises, the shrilling of crickets, the constant hum of cicadas, the sharp whistle of tree frogs. Suddenly Blake stopped her in her tracks.

'Just look,' he said.

'What is it?' she cried, enchanted. All over clumps of trees, small lights were flickering in and out. The result was fairylike.

'Fireflies,' said Blake. 'They're often in the bushes near to the beach.'

'It's magical,' she said.

His arm surrounded her and his hand tilted her chin so that their mouths were almost level. In the darkness she could see his eyes dark and glittering, and the outlines of his mouth, sensuous, curving. Hastily she drew away from him and his hand resumed its helpful grasp at her elbow as they continued walking.

'What a child you are, Gemma,' he said softly.

What does he mean? she thought. Does he think I'm a child because I indicated that I would refuse his kiss? Does he think that any other girl in this situation would have been glad of his embrace? She was shaken much more than she should have been by the small incident. I wanted him to kiss me, she thought. How could I?

Sea View was a collection of thatched round huts with one main building fronting on to the beach. There was a large long room, the dining-room area enclosed at one end, with small tables lit by candles with red shades. Most of the guests seemed to have dined already and were sitting around in the other room, some of them dancing to the soft background music coming from a loudspeaker. The waiter seated them in a corner where, beyond the undrawn curtains, one could glimpse the dark waves still. The loneliness of the scene outside seemed to emphasise the intimacy of the candlelit room with its red curtains and checked blue and white tablecloths. Shrimp cocktail was followed by fish fresh from the sea.

'Only caught this afternoon,' the waiter informed them.

'Poor things,' said Gemma. 'They could still have been swimming in that delicious sea.'

'But they're delicious themselves, don't you agree?'

'Yes, I suppose so. Certainly they taste very different from those bought from a fishmonger's slab.'

It seemed safe, she thought, to discuss the menu. She still felt shaken by the small encounter when they had seen the fireflies. She was making too much of it, perhaps. A kiss did not mean anything to a man like Blake. And it was her own fault, wasn't it, that she seemed to have some alarming physical reaction from even the slightest encounter with him? But she was safe enough this weekend, she thought. The shadow of Dion lay between herself and any other man.

'Would you like to dance?' he asked as they were finishing drinking their coffee.

'Do you think we should?'

She saw his swift frown.

'I brought you here to try to forget, for a while at least. You can't do any good to Dion by refusing to take a few steps on a dance floor, nor would he have wished it.'

Gemma stood up and accepted his embrace as they stepped out together on to the small polished surface where the other couples were turning slowly to the sounds of a taped slow waltz. She had not really been thinking of Dion, only of the effect of Blake's touch, the magnetic attraction of his hand upon her back, firm and strong. It seemed to have little to do with her opinion of the man himself. It must just be, she thought, that he has this physical attraction for women. It's something I've never encountered before, something I must be on my guard against.

But in the rosy candlelit twilight of the room, some strange emotion swept over her again as it had done that first night when she had danced with Blake at the little restaurant. She felt drawn to him by invisible threads as they moved around the room in silence, drawn by his dangerous attraction. She gathered together all her common sense to fight against this stupid emotion. How many other girls have felt just this? she thought. It must be that I've been relying on him too much during the past week and I'm mistaking my dependence for something else because I'm in need of comfort. I must learn to stand on my own feet again. If only I could get away!

'You're looking very solemn.'

She looked up at him and was painfully conscious of his dark penetrating gaze.

'Not at all. I'm enjoying the dance,' she said.

And so I am, and I wish it could go on for ever, drifting around in this hazy dream, not thinking of tomorrow or of that walk back to the cottage in the starlit darkness with Blake's hand on my arm and the temptation to be kissed.

Now the music changed to a tango and she had no time to think of anything else but the intricate steps as she followed Blake's guidance, but as she became used to his movements, the sensuous rhythm seemed to take over her body and they moved in a kind of harmony as if they were only one person. When the music ceased, there was a scattering of applause and, coming to herself, Gemma realised that they were the only couple left on the dance floor and that everyone else had been watching them. For Gemma the spell was broken.

'What do you say to a drink before we go?' asked Blake.

'I'd love something long and cool and non-intoxicating.'

'Lime juice and water and ice?'

'That sounds just wonderful!'

As she waited for him to bring the drink from the bar, a sweet-faced middle-aged woman sidled up to her.

'I loved the way you and your husband danced,' she said, 'Are you on your honeymoon?'

'Oh, no, no,' Gemma denied, 'nothing like that. We aren't married.'

'Not yet, I dare say, but you soon will be, I guess. You both look very much in love when you're dancing.'

How wrong can you be? thought Gemma.

'The tango just has that effect,' she told her companion.

By the time they were ready to leave, the moon had risen high in the dark blue sky, turning everything to silver.

'Shall we go back along the beach?' asked Blake. 'The tide's out and the sands will be dry by now.'

The night was very beautiful, utterly calm and still. A white gull flew over the moonlit waves and, in the seabush, fireflies twinkled like misplaced stars. The sand and the sea and the sky had a hazy blue look, and yet one could see everything quite clearly as the breakers pounded on the flat rocks and left them glistening and black where a moment before they had been covered with turbulent foam.

They had discarded their shoes and, as they walked in the dry silky white sand, small crabs like fragile ghosts of themselves scuttled away from them.

'It's all so lovely. I feel as if I'm in a dream,' said Gemma.

'Then keep on dreaming,' said Blake.

They had halted near the water's edge, and his arm, which had been on her elbow, now slid around and drew her to face him. His head came down, and then his mouth was on hers, firm and sensuous, just as she had known it would be. She forgot her doubts, for her whole body wanted to respond to this deep, beautiful embrace. It felt pliant as a willow wand under his touch and she wanted to be drawn nearer and nearer, to be lost in the moonlit magic of the night.

A wave swept over their feet, cold and like a warning, restoring her back to reality. She struggled away from him and he let her go without question. In the moonlight, his face looked dark and his expression was difficult to determine.

'Yes, I know, Gemma—I said I wasn't out to seduce you this weekend, and so be it. Let's say the moonlight made me a little drunk. In this kind of night you look too beautiful for your own good, do you know that?'

'I'd rather not know it,' said Gemma.

They continued their walk, but now for her the moonlit magic of the night held too much attraction. She felt drawn to Blake as if by a magnet and she longed to be in his arms again. But this was madness, she told herself, and if she gave way to these emotions, conjured up by the atmosphere of this lovely night, she would betray herself. Blake was the last person she would have chosen about whom to feel such sensuous emotion, and, if he knew how she felt, he would not be beyond taking advantage of it. She did not trust him, and now she did not trust herself.

Oh, this was all nonsense, she told herself. She had come here to Africa expecting love, and Dion, poor Dion, had not lived up to her expectations. So now her body was betraying her to the first man who showed some interest in her, a man, moreover, with whom she had to stay, for there was no way out of it.

The cottage was in darkness when they arrived there.

'I had intended to leave one of the lamps burning,' said Blake,' but the moonlight will light us to our beds.'

Moonlight flooded the little room, making everything appear unreal. Gemma stood near the table with the matchbox in her hand ready to light the lamp, wanting to get away from the silvery magic of the night, but as she lit the match, she felt Blake come up behind her and, stretching out his fingers, quench the little flame. Then his arms were around her, and she felt herself caught up against the hard tautness of his body, pressed against him so that for this moment nothing existed but his overwhelming physical attraction. His hands were caressing her skin where the sun-dress left her shoulders bare, then his face came down to kiss the curve of her neck and she felt the masculine roughness of his chin on the softness of her throat.

'Lovely Gemma,' he breathed.

As his hands slipped down the thin straps of her dress, she turned around and felt his kisses on the curve of her breasts, then on her mouth, gentle as a moth's touch at first but vigorous and demanding as her own passion responded, set on fire by the increasing urgency of his lovemaking. She felt she was like a blind creature that had been hidden for a long time in darkness, and now Blake's caresses were leading her towards some fantastic explosion of light.

'If only I could have felt like this with Dion,' she murmured to herself.

But he had heard Dion's name, for her lips were so close. She felt his body with all its urgent masculinity draw away from her. She swayed and would have fallen if his hands had not guided her to the sofa. And then he lit the lamp. By its light his expression was frozen and bleak.

'Go to bed, Gemma. I'm not prepared to be a substitute for a dead man, even if he hadn't been my friend. I wouldn't take advantage of the fact that you're missing Dion, and that if I made love to you, it would be him you would be imagining in my place. Isn't that true?'

She shrugged wearily. She wanted to deny what he had said, to tell him she had never felt this passion for Dion, now or in the past, but she was too ashamed to admit it. She did not want to feel passion for a man she hardly knew and whom in saner moments she did not even like. He must think I'm some kind of tramp, she thought, to respond to his lovemaking like that. What on earth possessed me?

She lay wakeful on her hard narrow bed until the cocks from the African huts began to crow in the early morning light, and she could hear the bed in the other room creaking occasionally under Blake's heavy frame as he too moved restlessly. Does he feel guilty too? she thought. After tonight, it makes it even more difficult to stay with him.

CHAPTER SIX

IT was as if the episodes in the moonlight had never happened. For the remaining time of the weekend, Blake was his usual cool, calm self. In fact to Gemma, grown used in the last week to expecting a certain kindness, he seemed very cold and aloof. Of course, she told herself, he had believed, when she said Dion's name, that she had been imagining it was he who was making love to her, and that was what had angered him. Well, let him go on thinking that. Much better that than that he should know the real reason, that she was physically responsive to him, Blake, in a way she had never known with Dion.

'Young madam look much better,' Shadrac commented approvingly when they returned.

It was true that the small pockmarked mirror of the cottage gave back a more golden image. Gradually her ivory skin was responding to the warm sun just as Blake had prophesied. He too noticed it when she sat down to breakfast the first morning after their return. She felt his dark penetrating gaze upon her now, the first time he seemed to have looked at her properly for some time. Indeed, he seemed to have been avoiding looking at her during the weekend, but now, back in his own home, the reserve he had used towards her seemed to have died down a little.

'Obviously the break did you good, Gemma,' he said. 'With that touch of sun, you're more beautiful than ever, just the kind of healthy, country look I need for my hostess at our set-up in the wine cellars.'

So there was nothing personal about his praise. He was just thinking of her appearance in connection with his business plans.

'Blake, let's get this straight,' she said. 'I'm not particularly interested in your ideas for improving the farm. I didn't know anything about these plans for my employment before I came here. Dion didn't even mention it, much less the fact that he'd signed a contract for me and that you'd paid my fare on the understanding that I would be willing to work for you. He only vaguely mentioned some light housekeeping. I realise now that I'm stuck here, but as soon as I can work off my debt to you, I'll consider myself a free agent. Dion had no right to sign a contract on my behalf.'

Blake grinned wryly.

'That's the first time I've heard you criticise him. But, Gemma, give it a try at least. I think you'll find the work interesting in spite of yourself, and by the time you've paid your debt, you won't want to leave, believe me.'

'Don't be too sure about that, Blake. Consider me a temporary employee. I feel obliged to stay now, but as soon as I can I'm going back to Britain. There's nothing to keep me here now.'

'Suit yourself, but at least give me a hand at getting this idea going. It means a lot to me.'

'What makes you think I can do it? I have no experience of this country and I don't know the first thing about a wine farm.'

'You will, you will, under my expert tuition, believe me, Gemma.'

How can I stay here, she thought, but how can I not?

'I'll give it a go,' she said. 'But don't blame me if it doesn't work out.'

'Certainly I'll blame you. My idea must succeed. I brought you out here because Dion assured me that you were the person to do it, and you only have to look around you to know how things have succeeded so far. I have all kinds of ideas for the farm. And another thing—I believe in getting value for my money. I didn't send for you with the idea that you were to marry Dion. I was given to understand that you were willing to do this work.'

'So we were both misled,' said Gemma. 'And I suppose I'll have to make the best of it now.'

'A willing best, I hope,' said Blake. 'I don't want any

unhappy faces around the cellars when the tourists arrive. That won't bring in the rands.'

'Is that all you think of? How much money you can make from the farm?'

'No, it isn't. I want to restore the farm to its former grace and beauty. I consider I've done quite a lot towards that so far. And it's your task to make it even better. I think in spite of everything, you'll enjoy doing that.'

'We'll see,' said Gemma.

'Now as regards where you're to live. Naturally I'll have to employ some kind of helper in Dion's place, and of course he'll have to have somewhere to live.'

'If you mean you want me to get out of the cottage, I'll do that willingly,' she told him.

Anything, she thought, to get away from those few short memories of Dion.

'Yes, I suppose it has rather painful memories for you. Would you consider living in the house?'

'No, thank you.'

His smile mocked her.

'I wonder why. No, don't tell me—it's better left unsaid. Well then, that leaves the Jonkershuis.'

'And what is that?'

'A small pretty building that was used in the old days to accommodate the young men of the family. I had it refurbished when the house was done, because we intend to show it to the tourists, but there are two rooms there with a bathroom and small kitchen. I had it renovated when I first came here, with the idea that it would maybe do for the staff one day. I'll show it to you. I think you could be quite comfortable there.'

From the moment Gemma saw her new accommodation, she fell in love with it. It had been some kind of loft and now was an apartment at the top of a curving external staircase. This led straight into a small room with light wood beams in the ceiling and a floor of light golden wood partly covered by handwoven rugs in brilliant colours. One or two easy chairs in blue linen looked old but comfortable, and the curtains were of some cream linen fabric with embroidered borders.

'I retrieved these from a chest in the attics,' Blake told her. 'Some industrious wife of my ancestors must have worked her eyes dim doing these by candlelight.'

A door led to the bedroom, a small room with a patchwork quilt in diamond pattern upon the brass bed, and a chest of drawers and small wardrobe in light yellow-wood. There was also a minute kitchen with blue and white plates on a small dresser and a tiny stove and fridge.

'You'd better tell me if anything's missing,' said Blake. 'I expect you'll be glad of a kitchen of your own now.'

He means I'm not to eat with him any more, thought Gemma. Well, in a way that's a relief, though I've got used to it, used to having breakfast on the patio to the sound of doves, with Blake sprawled in the opposite chair reading his mail or glancing through a newspaper. I expect he's glad to be rid of me.

The bathroom, though small, was pretty, with daffodil yellow tiles and an orange and yellow blind reflecting the sunshine.

'It all looks charming,' said Gemma.

'I was sure you'd like it. I used to stay here myself before my uncle died. A then girl-friend helped me with the decoration.'

'She had very good taste, then,' observed Gemma.

'Oh, yes, Trina knew what was suitable for any place, a humble apartment like this or a great house, though she was very good at spending money too, specially if it belonged to someone else.'

He sounds bitter, she thought. Trina? That was the name Dion had mentioned. She was the girl who let him down to marry someone rich, before he inherited the farm. I wonder where she is and if she regrets what she did now.

In the small apartment, Blake seemed too tall, too broad for his surroundings. Gemma was very conscious of him as they stood together examining the kitchen. If Trina was in love with him, she thought, it must have been hard to give him up. And Blake? She could not imagine him being in love, and yet Dion had said his girl-friend's action and her marriage to another man had hit him very hard. She can't have been truly in love, thought Gemma, or how could she have done it?

'Tomorrow I'll go over with you what I expect you to do, and we should be able to start quite soon. By that I mean we can start entertaining the public. We'll advertise in the Cape papers and possibly in Johannesburg as well. My idea is to use old Cape recipes for the restaurant, and we should be able to start a small shop to sell chutneys, cheeses, preserves, all made on the farm.'

'It all seems a bit ambitious,' Gemma commented. 'When do you propose we should open to the public?'

'Say next week.'

'Good heavens—next week! You expect rather a lot of me!'

'I should think you can do it. It will take your mind off other things.'

Strangely enough, when she had started on the schemes Blake explained to her, Gemma became interested in spite of all her doubts. It was such an attractive place in which to work. She would wake early in her small apartment high among the oak trees, hearing the birds sleepily chirruping at first and then awakening to their own vibrant song, rustling among the bright green leaves. Shadrac or one of the younger servants brought her coffee and hot croissants with preserve made of the sweet hanepoort grape. She hardly had to use her own little kitchen, and yet Blake made it plain that, now she was employed by him, he expected her to eat alone except when she was invited to the big house, and really she preferred this, for she was with Blake for a large part of the day while he instructed her in the way he expected her to run the catering side of his business, so she was relieved to be eating alone.

She still found his physical presence disturbing, and she found it hard to forget the strong emotions he had aroused in her during the weekend at the Wild Coast, but she told herself that she must blank her mind to that confusing memory, for when she thought of it it filled her with a kind of shame. I won't ever behave like that again, she vowed to herself. It was just the effects of the glamorous place, the dancing, the moonlight on the lonely beach. Here Blake is much more aloof, and I'm glad of it.

Already Blake had in his employment a little group of coloured girls who were able to make chutneys and preserves in the large kitchen he had provided next to the wine cellars. There was a dairy too where they made cheeses from the cream provided by a herd of gentle red and white cows.

'We'll start off simply with a cheese and wine lunch on small tables under the oak trees,' he said. 'Later we'll be more ambitious about providing Cape dishes, bobotie, chicken pie, *bredies*—that's a kind of stew cooked slowly. When the waterblommetjies are in season we can make it from those.'

'Hold on! Let me get started on the simple things first,' said Gemma.

'I have some old Cape books you can study. You'll soon get the hang of it. If you could qualify as a Cordon Bleu cook as Dion said you did, you can learn Cape Dutch cooking, I'm sure. The lunches will follow a tour of the cellars, I've had glasses made engraved with the Bienvenue symbol and these the tourists can keep after they've tasted the various wines. A nice touch, don't you think?'

'I suppose it is.'

'I'm certain it is. Most people like getting something extra for their money and this will be a souvenir they can take away. Also it will be an advertisement for us. If they offer their friends a drink in one of our glasses, that will lead to an explanation and description of the farm and what a visit here offers.'

'You think of everything, don't you?' she said drily.

'Certainly. That is why my schemes are usually a success.'

Gemma looked at the arrogant tilt of his chin, the curving confident smile of his mouth. This is when I like him least, she thought, when he's so pleased with himself. But even then she felt her own mouth responding in a smile. It was hard not to admit that certain charm of expression as he put his hand on her shoulder and bent down towards her, smiling into her eyes.

'Come and see my snow-white horses. That's another scheme I have in mind. There's an old Cape omnibus in the stables dating from 1870 and I propose to put it to use driving visitors around the grounds with my team.'

'You're sure you aren't thinking of importing a few lions and rhinos into the place to make a safari park?' smiled Gemma.

'I might at that, if I thought it would draw the crowds, but, no, I want the whole thing to be typical of the Cape tradition. It's a long time since lions roamed the hinterland. Let's leave them in the Kruger National Park, shall we? Now, come along. We'll have a break from figures and catering and go to see the stables.'

'But I was going to cost out those figures about the preserves.'

'Later, later. I want to show you my team.'

It's like living with a dynamo, she thought. When he's keen about something he's scheming he seems to give off sparks of electricity.

'Come along,' Blake said impatiently as he grasped her by the arm and hurried her along the path towards the stables. These were at the back of the house across a stone courtyard where oak trees gave shade and large wooden tubs of hydrangeas splayed out their great heads of blue and pink flowers. In the dim coolness of the white plastered building, a coloured man, wiry as a jockey, his face wrinkled like an old walnut, was polishing the brass upon some leather harness.

'Hi, Koos, *hoe gaan dit*—how goes it? Where are you, my beauties?' Blake cried, and was greeted by a musical descending whinny from a pair of equine throats.

'Oh, they're very fine,' said Gemma.

They were heavy carthorse types of mares but sturdy and beautiful, their coats silver-white and perfectly groomed. Their dark lovely eyes regarded Blake with immense interest.

'They seem to like you,' said Gemma, stepping aside

rather hastily as one of them dipped a large head in her direction.

'Of course they do. You adore me, don't you, Angélique? Wise girl, you know how to return affection.'

His long brown hand caressed the one horse and the other one nudged against him jealously.

'Oh, so you want some fussing too, do you? Just like a woman, aren't you? Only you must be the centre of attention. Come along, Gemma, don't stay in the background. Here's a piece of sugar for them—make friends with them that way. You'll have to get to know them while you're here. Why, you may even be required to drive them some day, who knows?'

Hesitantly Gemma put the sugar on to her outstretched hand. Not for the world would she show Blake that these huge animals so close to her were a new experience. Her hand felt rigid.

'You can't be frightened of them,' Blake accused her.

'Oh, no, of course not,' she said, stretching out her hand as the great head came nearer.

Soft as a feather, the mouth nuzzled her hand and the sugar was gone.

'Why, she's so gentle!' Gemma exclaimed.

'But Charmaine won't be if you don't give her a lump soon,' Blake warned her.

She felt a push that landed her against Blake. He steadied her with his hand as she hastily gave the sugar to the other mare, and when she had finished he did not let her go, but she found he had somehow drawn her away from the horses so that her back was against the white wall, near to the straw-filled manger, and his hands were now on each side of her, supported by the wall. Although she was not being touched by him now, yet it was almost as if she were in his embrace.

'Oh, Gemma, you're not as tough as you make out, are you? You were scared back there of those two gentle mares.'

'What nonsense! Indeed I wasn't,' Gemma denied indignantly.

'Then why are you trembling right now?'

'I'm not trembling.'

But she was. And it was not the mares that had caused this, even if they had contributed to it in the first place. It was because she was too near to him, near enough to kiss.

'Your eyes are so wide and blue. You look beautiful when you're just that tiny bit scared, Gemma. Right at this moment I could forget the vow I made that night at the Wild Coast.'

'What vow was that?' she murmured faintly.

'Never to try to make love to you again while you still remember Dion.'

'We both remember him,' said Gemma.

'Unfortunately yes, but sometimes I could wish to forget him, especially at moments like this.'

Why had he mentioned Dion? The feeling of guilt swept over Gemma again, clouding the new happiness she had begun to feel, and yet the memory of him was a safeguard protecting her from Blake and the emotion she felt when he was near to her.

Blake had employed a new man to take Dion's place. He was unmarried, a pleasant open-faced South African of Dutch extraction, his name Piet Viljoen, a man with a face reddened by the sun and bright blue eyes below the closely cropped brush of blond hair. He had been born on a wine farm but had wandered away from the country life in order to find his fortune in Johannesburg, the city of gold, but it had not worked out or come up to his expectations, and he was glad to get the work that Blake offered him.

'It sure feels good to be working for Mr Winfield,' he told Gemma. 'Working underground wasn't my scene, I discovered. Leave that to the moles, I say. And Mr Winfield is a ball of fire, isn't he? He certainly has done one wonderful job on this farm, by all accounts.'

'Oh, yes,' said Gemma, 'everyone seems to be agreed on that.'

More especially Mr Winfield, she thought to herself. I wish everyone didn't think he was so wonderful, she thought. It makes him so full of himself. I never did meet another man with so much ego! However, she had to admit his ideas worked when next week they set up their new tourist trap, as Blake called the scheme.

It was a beautiful day, clear, still and sunny enough for people to be attracted by the idea of a meal under the shade of the oak trees. Gemma had been up since dawn helping the waitresses with the preparation of the food. They were keeping it simple to begin with. The whole lunch was to be served on wooden boards, an attractive arrangement of different cheeses, newly baked bread made from stone-ground flour, twirls of butter, home-made salami, peach chutney, pickled onions, gherkins and cauliflower florets and decorative pieces of tomato and lettuce. But first there was the wine tasting, followed by a tour of the cellars, and Blake was to conduct the tour himself to begin with.

Gemma sat at the table in the entrance of the cellars, a large room with curved roof and wooden beams with old oak barrels around the walls. As the first group arrived for the tour, she accepted their money and then took her place behind the long curving bar that extended along one side of the room. Each guest had received coupons to cover the different kinds of wine they wished to taste, and they were obviously delighted to receive the bonus of a free glass so attractively decorated with the symbol of Bienvenue.

'What a cunning idea,' said one American lady with grey hair and sunglasses to her friend. 'The wine will sure taste good in one of these cute glasses.'

The amount of wine consumed was small and yet it gave the guests a chance to communicate with each other. A very friendly atmosphere was set up around the long bar and people who had only just met were talking to each other like old friends by the time Blake came to take them on their tour of the cellars where the wine was made.

There were some very attractive girls among the party, young and blonde, dressed in short sun-dresses, very abbreviated and revealing. Gemma noticed what an impression Blake's appearance made on these young things. They seemed to ignore her presence behind the bar and their comments were frank and loud.

'Isn't he dishy?' 'Gosh, where's he been all my life?' 'No go, Amanda, I saw him first!'

There was a lot of laughing and giggling as they proceeded to follow him to the cellars. Blake seemed to be lapping up their admiration, thought Gemma. He was smiling very charmingly down at them as they clustered around hanging on to his words, but quite evidently wishing they could hang on to him as well.

There you are, Gemma, she told herself. If you allowed any of the attraction you feel for Blake to show, you would just be one of the crowd like all the others. You must just keep your feet on the ground and never let him know that you've given his embraces a second thought. A good thing you have a lot to do, she admonished herself, and went into the large, picturesque room that was equipped as an old Cape kitchen with an open hearth, an old baking oven to the side, an antique yellow-wood table and many old-fashioned pieces of kitchen equipment such as they had used two hundred years ago in the early days of the settlement. Here the girls, dressed in sprigged ankle-length cotton dresses and pastel-coloured turbans, were arranging the food on to the wooden boards. Gemma went into the adjoining room that had more modern equipment in it and checked that the wine the guests might order was reaching a suitable temperature. Everything seemed to be going well.

'I hope lots of the tourists are going to stay for lunch,' she said to Katy, the head waitress.

'They are, they are. They are sitting under the oaks waiting for their wine.'

It was Blake who now strode in looking very pleased with himself.

'Have you got everything in order, Gemma?'

'Certainly,' she said. 'Katy, get the trays ready, please, and take the orders for the wine.'

'No, I'll do that myself and give everyone a little advice. That way I'll hope they'll want to take away some cases of the ones I recommend.'

'Very well, I'll help Katy with the cheese boards, then.'

'No, I'd prefer that you come with me and pick up some hints so you can do it yourself on days when I'm busy with other work,' said Blake.

'Do you trust me to know the wines to recommend, then?'

'No, but you'll learn. And naturally the better wines are the most expensive ones.'

'Of course. So I push those, is that it?'

'Yes, if you want to do good business. On the other hand, if your clients are young and ignorant perhaps it would be better policy to let them drink the less expensive wines. That way they'll recommend the place to their friends and come back.'

'And you'll get more of their admiration,' Gemma could not resist saying.

'Oh, you noticed that? Well, it's all good for our trade using a little charisma, isn't it?'

'Is that what you call it?' asked Gemma.

Whatever it is, he's using it to the full, she thought, as she followed him around the tables. His charm works on all these people—and doesn't he know it too!

One of the pretty blondes spoke to her as she served the wine at her table.

'It must be wonderful to work for a man like Mr Winfield. I'd absolutely adore it. Aren't you fortunate?'

'It would appear so,' said Gemma.

Her ironical tone was lost on the pretty tourist.

No sooner had the lunch party left than another set of tourists arrived, keen to sample the wine and go over the cool cellars in the sleepy heat of the afternoon. Gemma's body was beginning to feel the strain.

'You must have a constitution of steel,' she said to Blake as he poured wine and chatted up the younger, prettier tourists, not forgetting a word to charm the blue rinse brigade as well.

'I have, I suppose. Not to worry. Only a couple more hours and you can put your feet up.'

But in the meantime there was the tea and coffee to prepare, the fresh scones with dollops of cream and home-made preserves, the *koeksusters*, delicious plaited confections dipped in syrup and then deep-fried to a tempting colour of gold, the *melkterte*, in their pastry cases, light as a soufflé, made from butter, eggs, milk and flour with a cinnamon topping.

As the sun approached the west, the last of the visitors departed, and at last Gemma was able to collapse into a chair.

'Don't do that,' said Blake. 'You won't want to get up again. Are you shattered? Go and have a shower and come to the house for dinner—we deserve some kind of celebration.'

Gemma looked rather resentfully at Blake, who seemed to look as spruce as when he had started this morning. How does he do it? she thought. Of course he's so carried along by the fact that his scheme seems to be turning out well, that he must get extra spurts of adrenalin from that fact. It means a lot to him, naturally. Much more than it does to me.

And yet, in spite of her weariness, as she stood under the shower, letting the cool water lave her tired body in the small primrose-coloured bathroom, she could not help feeling pleased that all their plans seemed to have worked well. Her pale green dress brought memories of that weekend, but it could not be helped. Even though there were faint lilac shadows under her eyes, the dress was still becoming to her pale golden skin and red-gold hair. For once she applied a little blusher, very carefully and delicately. She was determined she would not look shattered, as Blake had put it. She must show that she could hold her own in this new scheme. She took great care to arrange her hair becomingly, twisting it up into a knot and letting wisps of curls escape over her brow and on each side of her face.

Under the old vine with its twisted stems that wound on pillars by the side of the house, there was a striped swinging seat, beside the wrought iron white-painted table, and here she found Blake, sitting idly relaxed and looking as if he had done nothing more arduous all day than go for a swim or play a round of golf. He was wearing a cream-coloured safari suit and the immaculately tailored jacket was open to the waist, exposing the bronze muscles of his chest. In the green shade of the vine stood a wine bucket on a stand and, in a bed of ice, there was a bottle with a gold foil.

'French champagne tonight, what do you say? I don't often patronise a foreign wine, but there are occasions when nothing else will serve. No, don't choose that hard chair. Come and sit over here with me, you'll find it much more comfortable.'

As Gemma sank into the soft cushions of the swinging seat, her tiredness seemed to vanish. In its place was a completely relaxed, happy sensation, and, when Blake gave her a slender, tall glass of the golden sparkling liquid, she sipped it appreciatively.

'How do you think things went today?' he asked her.

'Very well on the whole. We'll be quicker with the service when the girls are more used to it.'

Together they went over the events of the day. She had expected some criticism, but, if he had any, he was saving it until later.

'You did pretty well for a first attempt,' he told her. 'Dion was right. In spite of the doubts I originally had about you, you'll do fine for this job.'

'But I still intend to go, just as soon as I can manage it,' Gemma told him.

'I wonder why.'

'Could be your charisma doesn't work as well for me as for some others,' said Gemma.

'No? That's a damn challenging thing to say. Puts a man on his mettle!'

Just as well, thought Gemma, if he thinks his charm doesn't affect me. She glanced at him. He was far too close sitting near her in this swinging seat. There was something most voluptuous about the sensation of being lapped in the soft cushions and lazily moving to and fro in the scented blue of the evening. His hand was along the back of the seat and now she was vividly aware of her own satiny smooth skin beneath his fingers as he stroked her shoulder and the upper part of her arm. A dangerous thrill invaded her body, a breathless kind of emotion that she had felt before and recognised as part of the attraction he held for her.

She felt she should shrug away that hand from her

arm before she betrayed what she was feeling, and yet there was something so captivating about this situation, and she was seized with a delicious languor. She felt she could stay like this for a very long time, held and yet not held in Blake's arms, swinging and being sensuously stroked, while a large yellow moon rose slowly in the deep blue of the heavens over the white gables of the house and the scent of frangipani came upon the evening breeze.

'So, Gemma, my charisma only puts you to sleep,' she heard Blake say.

She seemed to come back from some place very far away.

'Perhaps. Does that disappoint you?'

'Certainly. I'm used to better results than that. Come on, I'll call Shadrac to serve dinner. It seems to me the only desire you're going to feel tonight is the desire for your bed.'

'What else did you expect?'

'Oh, one can always hope,' he shrugged. 'Given the situation, glamorous night, man and woman alone in the moonlight, there could be a fitting climax to a successful day. But not with you, Gemma. You always have your emotions well under control, isn't that so?'

'I hope so.'

How little he knows, she thought. Well, I should be thankful, I suppose, that he hasn't detected the fact that his physical attraction works on me as much as it does on any young teenager, but I have the ability to hide it and I must continue to do just that.

Shadrac had prepared a light supper of chilled soup, creamed chicken tasting delicately of tarragon and lemon, and a refreshing salad made from a variety of exotic fruits. It was served, not in the large central dining room but in a small intimate room with a tiny folding table and two chairs. The walls of the room were of an old rose colour, and Gemma wondered how many women had dined with Blake in these surroundings. The night had become cooler and Shadrac had lit logs and pine cones in the cast-iron basket that was backed in the fireplace by an intricately moulded fireback with a pattern of grapes. There was a silver candlestick and a rose-coloured lamp in a corner of the room, and there was no other light except that of the fire, so that for Gemma it seemed like being inside a pink shell.

She could not help noticing that, in spite of the fact that the table and chairs were quite small, the only other furniture, apart from a corner cupboard in which there was some china, and some fitted bookcases against the wall, was a large settee that seemed to take up all the space in front of the fire, and when Shadrac served the coffee and bade them goodnight, there was no choice but to sit on this settee next to Blake. It was as soft and almost as seductive as the swinging seat on the patio, she thought.

'You do go in for very comfortable furniture,' she commented.

'Glad you like it. Unlike my ancestors, I believe in luxury, especially when I'm entertaining a woman. No hard benches with opsit candles for me.'

'What do you mean?' she queried.

'I expect you haven't heard of the custom. In early settler days, when a man went courting a young *meisie* he'd set his heart on, she lit a candle and he could stay as long as the light lasted. If she favoured his suit, he could expect a longer candle than usual, I guess. What do you say, Gemma? Shall we douse the lamp and find out how long this candle lasts?'

'But I'm in your home, not you in mine, so I can leave at any time I choose, can't I?'

'But you don't choose to leave just yet, do you? Why, Gemma, you've taken on a new lease of life. Your eyes are sparkling like sapphires. It must be the champagne. I don't flatter myself that it could be my company—or could it?'

He took her two hands and turned her around to face him.

'Let me look at you. Yes, that touch of the sun has given you a lovely golden glow. You really are a beautiful creature, Gemma. Why waste time on grieving? We know only too well that Dion has gone forever. Nothing can bring him back.'

His arms were around her now and his hand curved around the nape of her neck drawing her towards him. She closed her eyes and felt his fingers tracing the curve of her throat, then upwards to her mouth where they outlined its shape, so soft and vulnerable. And then Blake was kissing her, slowly and almost languidly at first, kisses like the soft moths that were fluttering against the window, drawn by the lamplight. She felt her lips part under his and the kisses that had been so gentle became hard and fiercely passionate. His hands sought her breasts and she felt the weakness and the strength of her own sensual desire. She was being carried away now on a tide as relentless as the waves of that other dark sea, but he was there beside her as he had been then and their breath mingled in hesitant whispers as if for both of them their kindled passion was almost too much to bear. I'm committed to him now, she thought wildly. There can be no going back.

Like some sound from another world, the door bell clanged out its loud metallic summons.

'Forget it, Gemma,' Blake murmured against her mouth. 'Ignore it, and whoever it is will go away.'

But the sound had broken the spell. Her heart was pounding madly, yet she knew she could not possibly ignore the fact that someone stood on the other side of that heavy door, someone who sought entrance into this room that a moment ago had seemed like Paradise.

'Why be nervous, my dear? You look as if there might be a ghost at the door. It's probably just some employee with something that can easily wait until tomorrow. We certainly don't need any intruders now, do we?'

The bell rang again, echoing through the high rooms with startling clamour.

'You should go, Blake,' she urged. 'Whoever it is means to see you.'

'Stay right here, Gemma. Promise me you'll be waiting for me when I've got rid of whoever is there.'

But she made no promises. Already she was regretting the fact that she had been so overwhelmed by his undoubted attraction. What a fool I am, she thought. What can he think of me?

As Blake went reluctantly to the door, she stood up and looked into the gilt mirror that hung over the fireplace. As she tried to smooth her hair, she was startled by the radiance of her expression. Was that because the room reflected its colouring in a flattering, rosy glow? A log fell from the fire and she busied herself putting it back with the silver tongs from the old set of fireirons left there for that purpose. So she did not hear the door open, nor realise that two people had entered the little room.

'Have I interrupted something, Blake? I must say you two look as if you've been making yourselves very cosy here!'

As she rose to her feet, Gemma saw the person Blake had named the intruder. In the golden glow of the candlelight, she seemed to her the most beautiful creature she had ever seen, with melting dark eyes, shining black hair almost to her waist, and a willowy, curving figure set off by a figure-hugging dress of cream jersey. Diamonds sparkled at her ears and throat and a gold charm bracelet tinkled on her wrist. Her high-heeled strappy gold sandals made scarcely any sound as she came towards Gemma with extended hands.

'Blake tells me you've been a great help to him today. Unfortunately I couldn't make it for the opening of his new scheme, but I was determined to get here somehow when I saw the advertisement in the newspaper. Aren't you going to introduce us, Blake? I'm Trina van Zyl. I had to come here to see if I could be of any assistance. Blake and I have always been devoted to each other, haven't we, Blake?'

CHAPTER SEVEN

'BLAKE tells me you intend to leave here and go back to Britain quite soon.'

Some tiny devil prompted Gemma to say, 'Oh, no, my plans are quite flexible. In fact I like it so much here I might easily decide to stay. The work is very interesting and the surroundings so beautiful, and I have excellent accommodation—thanks, I believe, to you.'

A swift frown marred the perfect beauty of Trina's face.

'I arranged that for Blake. It was a retreat from the house when his uncle was alive. We spent many happy hours there.'

Now, Gemma thought, she would visualise all too well the picture of Blake and Trina using her beautiful little apartment in the Jonkershuis as a place where they could be alone, and, if they were alone, it could only have had one purpose, that they could make love. What happened then has nothing to do with me now, she told herself, and, from the night Trina arrived, you made up your mind that there was to be no more nonsense about surrendering yourself to Blake's physical attraction. He's not for you. But is he for Trina? Surely Trina has a husband, even if he isn't in evidence.

That night, two weeks ago, she had swiftly made some excuse to leave them, but she could not sleep, and although she had not intended to spy on them, she had heard Trina's car driving away in the early hours. Well, at least she was not staying with Blake. She had leased a holiday apartment at Camp's Bay along the coast. Gemma supposed she had to be discreet, but she was at Bienvenue just about every day, acting as if she were in charge of the whole proceedings. She had taken over from Gemma at the bar, encouraging the visitors to taste and buy the wine and, of course, Blake obviously thought she was doing a wonderful job. Gemma seemed to get relegated to the kitchen and to the less interesting work, and Blake did not seem to notice. As long as his precious scheme goes well, he doesn't care what happens, she thought. Gemma was not the type to take this kind of thing lying down, but it seemed a losing battle. Whenever any little thing went wrong, and naturally it was not all plain sailing at first, she seemed to be on the receiving end for the blame.

One day there was a complaint because Trina had given a customer the wrong kind of wine when he had ordered some other kind. The customer complained to Blake, who came to Gemma in the kitchen.

'Gemma, why on earth did you give this man the red wine when he specifically told you he liked white? He said it was recommended as being something he would prefer, and now he has had the trouble of bringing it back. The least I can do is to offer to refund his fuel costs for the journey.'

'But I haven't had anything to do with the wine orders lately,' protested Gemma, 'Trina has taken over. She's been doing it all.'

'Nonsense! Trina would never make a mistake like that. She knows about wines, and I'm beginning to think you don't, if you make stupid mistakes like that.'

'I don't have much chance of knowing about wines if you don't give me any further instruction, do I? I thought the idea was that I should go around with you listening to your conversation with the customers, but lately I don't seem to be able to do so.'

'Do I detect a little green-eyed jealousy in that remark?' he drawled.

'Certainly not, but I am anxious to do my job properly, and I hate to be frustrated and accused of not doing it well.'

'You could learn a great deal from Trina, instead of being so dog-in-the-mangerish about her. While she's here she may as well use her talent for charming the tourists. She won't be here for ever.'

'I should hope not,' said Gemma.

'Really, Gemma, I had no idea you were so spiteful—

and do something about your hair if you're going to serve lunch later.'

He turned and walked out. Gemma was standing over the hot coal stove because she had thought while she had some time on her hands she would try some old Cape recipes. She felt thoroughly exasperated, and the heat of the stove did nothing to decrease her annoyance. She could feel perspiration trickling down her legs and her hair hung limp about her face. No wonder he doesn't take me around to charm the customers looking like this, she thought, but why should I be blamed for Trina's mistakes? And why has she come back? I wouldn't have thought Blake would want anything to do with a woman who's rejected him once, but, according to Dion, she was the only woman that Blake had ever wanted to marry, and certainly she's terribly attractive physically, and that's all he seems to care about.

There were no more dinners in the intimate dining room, or drinks on the patio. From the moment she arrived Trina seemed to have taken Blake over entirely. The silver Mercedes went out at about seven or eight in the evening and did not return until some time in the early hours. Gemma knew this, for she sometimes lay restless in her bed, seeing the moonlight reflecting the shadows of leaves, hearing the eerie calls of the curlews in the lands and not able to recapture sleep. And she was troubled by nightmares. When she slept, she often had the recurring dream about the scene of Dion's death.

At this time Gemma was grateful for the company of the new assistant, Piet Viljoen. She saw much less of Blake because Trina was always with him, but she saw much more of Piet because he seemed to seize the opportunity to be in her company. He was often around helping her when there were orders to be checked or heavy things to carry into the kitchen. He was dull and ordinary and dependable, and she liked him, because he was a complete contrast to Blake, who could make you feel over the moon one moment and just as easily cast you down into the depths again. So when he started dating her, she accepted his attentions.

There was no trade at the wine farm on a Sunday, and when they were both free, she and Piet would go off in his old Chevrolet and find some sheltered beach to bathe and have a picnic lunch. The resorts were always crowded at the weekend, so that there was no question of lovemaking. He was a slow stolid man and seemed to treat her as he would a sister, and for this she was very thankful. She felt she had had enough of feeling physical attraction for a man she hardly liked. She did not mind the brief caresses that Piet gave her so long as he didn't follow them up, and for the moment he showed no sign of doing so. Nevertheless Blake seemed to have noticed Piet's interest in Gemma. One day, when he was helping Gemma with something, Blake came in and said, 'You seem to be spending a lot of time in the kitchen, Piet. I wonder why. I never said domestic work was part of your job.'

Piet looked abashed.

'The old preserving pans are pretty heavy. I was helping Gemma to handle them.'

'And taking the opportunity to handle Gemma as well, it seems!'

They had both had hold of the handle and she supposed he had seen their hands touching, nevertheless Gemma felt furious that Blake should be so unreasonable over such a small thing.

'I had no intention of keeping Piet from his work,' she protested, 'but Trina has taken my kitchen helpers to work in the cellar.'

'Well, Piet is needed now for supervising the spraying,' said Blake, and Piet left hurriedly, glad no doubt to be out of the storm that seemed to be brewing.

'You're very unreasonable about Trina, I've noticed,' Blake told her. 'You seize on the opportunity to blame her when obviously Piet is hanging around here just to make a pass at you and you know it.'

'I know no such thing!' she retorted. 'Since Trina arrived, I'm not able to do my job as well as I would like because I get a lot of interference and not as much help as I had before.'

'Always Trina is blamed for your own shortcomings! Really, Gemma, I would have thought you'd be ashamed to show such jealousy so openly.'

'Why should I be jealous?'

Gemma was furious that he should think her jealous because he was paying so much attention to Trina.

'Why indeed? But, Gemma, if you'd be sensible on the subject of Trina, she could teach you about this work, but you seem so obstinate that she never gets the chance. She told me so herself.'

'Indeed? I thought I was employed to work for you, not for Trina.'

'You disappoint me, Gemma. You've taken a childish dislike to someone who only has your interests and the interests of the farm at heart, and you know how much that means to me—or do you know? You've emphasised right from the start that you intend to go back to the United Kingdom as soon as you're able. What interest can you possibly have in the farm when you have that object in mind all the time?'

Gemma wanted to tell Blake that she had changed her mind, that, now she had lived here for some time, she could not imagine living anywhere else, and that, in spite of all her troubles, she loved Bienvenue more than any other place, but she could not tell him that. It would seem that she was trying to find favour with him just as Trina did.

Then one day suddenly it seemed that Trina was leaving, and she did not seem too pleased about this fact either. In the evening, as Gemma was preparing to cook an omelette for her supper, she heard the rattle of Trina's high heels on the outside staircase, and in a moment Trina swept in, not bothering to knock. The white suit and emerald sweater she wore suited her dark beauty. An emerald and diamond bracelet clasped her wrist and tiny emeralds swung and glittered on each ear.

'I have to go tomorrow. It's all rather tiresome. It seems my husband needs me for some big affair, a business dinner that's taking place in Johannesburg. However, I think I've given Blake a good start with his scheme for selling wines, better than he would have had if I hadn't come.'

Gemma could not bring herself to agree with this.

'We seemed to be doing very well from the start,' she said.

'Of course. Blake has a way with him, as no doubt you've noticed, but it takes a woman to give it a personal touch, and one could hardly have expected you to know about wines when you were only just out of the U.K., could you?'

'I do happen to know something about wines,' Gemma contradicted. 'I've been in the catering trade and worked in pretty high class restaurants, but of course I had to get to know about the wines produced here. I was just doing so when you arrived.'

And took over, she added to herself.

'Oh, naturally Blake was making the best of things before I came. He could hardly have turned you away after what happened to Dion, could he?'

While Trina was talking, her eyes were roving around the room, and now she stood up and started handling a small green malachite rhino that stood on the mantel.

'Oh, good, Blake still has this. It was a memento of a trip we took to a game reserve in Zululand. I bought one for him and he bought one for me.'

Gemma found herself excessively and perhaps unreasonably irritated by the way in which Trina's long scarlet-tipped fingers handled the little sculpture. She put it down, but then proceeded to wander around the room, handling the different objects as if they belonged to her.

'I don't blame you for wanting to get away,' she said, in spite of the fact that Gemma had said she might stay. I don't believe she listens to anything anyone else says, Gemma thought. She is completely absorbed in her own effect on people.

'I wonder you were able to stay on at all after the awful thing that happened to Dion.'

'I had to stay,' Gemma said flatly. 'I couldn't afford to go home straight away.'

She did not want to tell Trina that Blake had paid for

her fare, but now Trina said, 'I'm sure Blake would have lent you the money if you'd asked him. It probably didn't occur to him. He's only trying to be kind giving you a job here when really you know absolutely nothing about wines and the kind of catering this place needs.'

'I've had a great deal of experience in catering. Blake seemed quite satisfied with my qualifications.'

'Ah, but it's the practice of them that counts, isn't it? That, and a certain amount of personality. However I don't suppose you'll be here for long. Blake must have people about him who are expert if he's going to make a go of the tourist side of the farm. That's why he was so glad to have me here.'

'And now you have to go. Well, we'll all have to do our best to manage without you, won't we?'

Gemma was ashamed of her own sarcasm, but in any case it was lost on Trina, who had the knack of making her furious.

'Oh, don't worry, I'll be back soon, as soon as I can manage it, but perhaps by then you'll have gone. I don't know how you can bear to stay here after what happened. I couldn't have done it, but then I'm so sensitive. If I'd truly loved someone, I couldn't have gone on living in the same place just as if nothing had happened. You must have a very strong personality to do that, or else you didn't love him as much as you'd thought when you decided to come here.'

There was too much truth in Trina's remarks for Gemma's comfort, even if she was trying to needle her. She felt a wave of guilt wash over her again. Why had she stayed here if not because she felt some strong attraction to Blake? If she had had any sense, she would have tried to get a job elsewhere and paid him back that way, but, until Trina came, she had been prepared to settle down in this work and she had loved her little apartment. She still had bad dreams about Dion but she would have had those anywhere, she thought.

'How I felt about Dion is my own affair, Trina,' she said now. 'Nothing can bring him back, however much I mourn.'

'It's good you're so levelheaded, but if you take my

advice, you'll get away from here. Blake's not usually charitable, but he must feel some responsibility for you because of Dion.'

'There's no need for him to feel like that, and if he wants me to go, he can tell me himself. Have you discussed all this with Blake?'

'Naturally,' shrugged Trina.

'And did he say he wanted me to go?'

Trina looked away. She smoothed the round green flank of the rhino sculpture.

'I wouldn't like to say.'

So Blake did want her to leave. Well, she would confront him herself over this. He had no right to use Trina of all people as a go-between. Suddenly Trina seemed nervous. She stopped her jittery roaming around the little room and took up the emerald lizard purse that exactly matched her high-heeled strappy sandals.

'Well, Gemma, nice knowing you. I must fly now. Blake's taking me to the airport and returning my hired car for me. If you feel like getting a job in Johannesburg any time, do get in touch with me.'

That's the last thing I'll ever do, thought Gemma, as she heard the high heels going tap, tap, tap down the old staircase. She went back to her omelette, but by this time it looked as flat and tired as she herself felt.

But once Trina had gone, it was as if the sun had come out again from behind a cloud. At least, it was like that for Gemma, even though she thought that Blake seemed more irritable than usual, and she put this down to the fact that he was missing Trina. She had wished to ask him if he really wanted her to leave, but for some time she did not seem to get the opportunity. He was busy with Piet and the business of the farm, and she was hard at work making up for the time when Trina had excluded her from the study and sale of the wine. In this Piet was able to help her and she began to ask his advice rather than rely too much on Blake, who seemed preoccupied with his thoughts. But one day just as there was a lull in the spate of tourists, Blake came in to see her.

'There's been an invitation to a dinner from a company connected with the wine business. I think you'd better come with me, Gemma—it will give you an opportunity to learn something more about it, maybe. It's to be rather a formal affair, black tie for me and for you a long dress, I suppose.'

Gemma was surprised by his casual offer that she should accompany him although, since Trina had departed, she supposed it was to be expected that he would ask her, since he was so keen she should get to know about wines.

'I haven't a long dress,' she stammered, somewhat taken aback by his abrupt invitation. Invitation? It was more in the nature of a command.

'What about the dress you brought with you? You won't be needing it now, will you?'

She thought it cruel and unkind of him to remind her about the wedding dress, but it did not mean the same to him as it had meant to her, of course. That night, before she went to bed, she got it out and tried it on. Yes, it was a lovely dress, and it was not as if it had been specially made for her own wedding. Bridget would not mind if she used it for the dinner. It had been made with a long-sleeved silk jacket that could be taken off and then the dress was transformed into an evening dress, less formal than the first version. It transformed her too. She looked taller and slimmer and more beautiful in the intricately embroidered gown. It was certainly good enough for any event. She would wear it and not think of what might have been.

Now that they were alone again and she was more in his company, she became uneasily aware that for her Blake still held an intense physical attraction. When he breezed into the kitchen, joking with the hired girls, tasting the cheeses and preserves, sampling the wine, there was little of that previous dislike of him and yet he could still exasperate her with his arrogance. And he knew it. He liked to tease her in front of the assistants, who would pretend to be shocked at his banter. Katy thought he was wonderful.

'If I were you, Miss Gemma, I'd try to get the baas,'

she advised. 'That Missus Trina, she's spoken for, isn't she, because she has a husband? She has no right to come here making up to Mr Blake. She's a bad one, that.'

'I don't think he'd have me, Katy,' smiled Gemma.

'I think he would. It would take a clever woman to get the master, but you are very clever, Miss Gemma.'

'I'm glad you think so, Katy.'

Sometimes when he was in the kitchen, Katy would try her idea of a gentle prodding.

'The baas needs a wife, not so? Every man must get a wife some time. Why doesn't the baas look around and find one? No good running after married women.'

Gemma thought Katy's straight talking might annoy Blake, but he merely laughed and appeared to agree with her.

'Yes, Katy, you're right. I do need a wife, but where am I to find one? Who would have me?'

'Someone not a thousand miles away, I dare say,' said Katy, glancing slyly at Blake and then at Gemma.

Blake laughed, and Gemma's heart gave a stupid jolt at the sight of him so relaxed and smiling.

'So that's your little plan, Katy, is it? But she doesn't appreciate me as much as you do, unfortunately.'

I'm glad he thinks that, thought Gemma. He must never know how attractive I find him in spite of all his faults.

He had asked her to come to dinner at his house several times, but she always found some excuse, because she dreaded being alone with him. How could she be restrained with him if he made love to her, when even the touch of his hand on her arm, as they consulted with each other over the wine bar, sent a tingling thrill through her body? I should get away, she thought. Soon I'll have enough saved to repay him the fare, and then I can save to pay for my return to Britain. He wants to get rid of me—Trina said so. But can I believe her? Since she left he seems more pleasant to me, and yet there's something on his mind. When he isn't aware that I'm looking at him, he frowns as if he has some worry. Maybe he has. Maybe since Trina has come back into his life, he has found he still loves her.

Piet had noticed something too.

'What's biting Blake, Gemma?' he asked. 'Is he overworking, do you think, trying to run the wine farm and the catering side as well?'

'I shouldn't think so, Piet. He always seems to have the strength of a lion.'

'And the whole thing is running smoothly, it seems. Could he have money worries?'

'I don't know anything about that, Piet.'

'It hardly seems likely. The farm's prosperous and getting more so. Is it that woman, do you think? Is he too involved with her?'

'He would hardly confide in me about that, would he?'

'I understand she is married still,' Piet mused. 'Maybe that's what's bugging him. I must admit she seems to have everything it takes. What a beauty she is! She seems to be very keen on him and he on her, don't you think?'

Gemma was surprised at the shaft of pain that seemed to pierce her heart.

'I don't want to gossip about Blake,' she said sharply.

He looked hurt, as well he might, by her frigid tone.

'I didn't mean to gossip, but surely it must be of some interest to you? Blake is such an impressive personality, it's fascinating to speculate on what makes him tick. But I can tell you this much—something is getting him down at the moment, and I don't know what it is.'

Later, lying in her bed under the patchwork counterpane, hearing the sleepy murmur of birds in the trees outside her window, Gemma tried to think clearly. Why did I feel so much pain, she thought, when Piet spoke of Blake and Trina? I couldn't be in love with him myself, could I? She tried to dismiss the crazy idea from her mind, but it began to gain ground. I disliked him from the first day, she thought, so how could this be? Lately, in spite of his frowns and worries, he has still found time to be charming to me, praising my work, complimenting me on my appearance. Why is he doing this if not to try to fascinate me with his so-called charisma, and is it because I told him it doesn't work with me? But it does. Oh, Gemma, what a fool you are! You've fallen in love with your boss, just like all the rest, and he's in love with Trina—I'm sure of it. One thing's certain: I must get away from here.

She looked forward with a mixture of dread and delight to the night of the dinner. She had taken such care never to be alone with Blake lately, and now she was going to spend a whole evening in his company. But there would be other people there, so why should she worry?

She made her preparations almost as if the wedding dress was to be used for the purpose for which it was made.

'If you want to have your hair set, Piet is going in to town and can take you,' Blake had told her, rather to her surprise. He must think I need it, she told herself wryly.

'But what about the visitors?' she queried.

'Katy and I can cope for once,' said Blake.

Piet dropped her at one of the big shopping centres on the outskirts of the town and she spent a luxurious couple of hours spending money that she had been determined to save. The hairdresser was quite excited by her unusual shade of red-gold hair and invented an intricate, sophisticated style for her when she told him it was for a special occasion. She also had a manicure, her pretty filbert nails lacquered in a shade of peach. The wedding dress was not white but a deep shade of cream silk, and she bought peach-toned make-up to compliment it, apricot lipstick and an eyeshadow in a shimmering golden brown. The cream satin shoes to go with the dress would not be suitable in these circumstances, so she rather reluctantly bought a pair of gold high-heeled sandals. I'm quite mad, she thought, spending some of my savings just to look beautiful for this one night. However, I didn't have to buy a dress. Like Cinderella, I'll wake up to reality when the night is over, but at least the Fairy Godmother supplied the glass slippers. I've had to buy my own!

Blake had not asked her to go to the house first as

she had thought he might. She had both feared and desired the idea of being alone with him once more in that intimate little room, but he said he would call for her at the Jonkershuis and they would go straight to the hotel where the event was to be held.

She bathed in a leisurely fashion in bathwater scented with lemon verbena, then powdered lavishly and slipped on the gossamer tights and tiny satin and lace briefs that were the only underwear she needed under the lovely dress. The shimmering new make-up emphasised her shining eyes, her radiant expression. I shouldn't look so excited, she thought. Blake is sure to notice; he doesn't miss a trick.

The parchment silk of the dress enhanced her golden colouring, and when she looked into the mirror, she could not believe this stranger with the bronze-gold hair and the honey skin and the dreamy blue eyes was really herself. A topaz pendant on a golden chain swung over the low cut of the bodice, that showed the creamy curves of her small breasts beneath the gold of her neck and gleaming shoulders. The bodice made her waist look so tiny, doll-like, further emphasised by the silky parchment folds of the billowing skirt.

For a while, as she stood at the window waiting for Blake, she experienced a feeling of profound sadness. This should have been the dress for her wedding. Oh, Dion, she thought, why did everything go wrong? And now I'm fatally attracted to someone who doesn't love me. What a tangle it all is! It would have been better if I'd never come here.

But when she opened the door to Blake, everything seemed to vanish from her mind except an overwhelming emotion at the sight of him. She had never before seen him in formal dress, and now the dark suit and snow-white shirt with its black tie enhanced his good looks. How handsome he is, she thought. No wonder women seem to adore him. And why should I now join the crowd? Oh, Gemma, after tonight you must get over this madness, but tonight you can indulge your folly and imagine for a short while that anything could be possible.

'Gemma, how lovely you look! What have you done to yourself? Certainly you'll be the most beautiful woman at the dinner. I feel I hardly dare touch you or I might undo some of all this glamour!'

But Blake took her arm as he guided her down the curving outer staircase, and again she felt that sharp thrill running through her veins like quicksilver. When they had settled themselves in the silver-grey cushions of the car, he casually tossed a cellophane box across at her. It was tied with a satin bow and through the transparent bubble of the box she could see a most perfect orchid, almost the same colour as the topaz at her breast.

'I remembered your dress was cream,' said Blake, 'so the usual purple or white cattleya wouldn't suit it.'

Gemma was surprised at his careful choice and the fact that he had held a memory of the dress.

'It's glorious,' she said, 'like very fine velvet. I hardly dare wear such a thing.'

'Nonsense—take it out. The florist has provided some kind of fastening, I believe.'

He watched her as she tried to pin the perfect bloom on to the top of her dress. Her fingers trembled and she felt clumsy and afraid to spoil the lovely flower.

'Let me do it for you,' he said, and took the orchid from her hand.

The long, slender brown fingers touched her breast as he pinned it on to the curving neck of the low-cut gown. Gemma tried to appear unaware of it but her heart was beating madly and she was sure he must notice.

'There, it looks beautiful, just like its wearer.'

His head came down and he kissed the place above the orchid where the fragrant hollow showed between the creamy curves of her breasts.

'Shouldn't we be going?' she asked tremulously.

His lips curved in that smile that could sometimes be cruel and yet now charmed her entirely.

'I never saw any woman whose eyes could look so blue and huge and extremely alarmed! Come on, Gemma, you must enjoy this evening—I insist on it. Don't look at me as if I'm some kind of ogre.'

'I'm not. I do intend to enjoy it. Let's not quarrel tonight, Blake.'

'I won't quarrel with you at all if in exchange you promise to forget the past for once.'

By that he means Dion, thought Gemma. But Dion is only a sad memory to me. I know now that I never loved him. However, it's best that Blake should think I did. Anything is better than his knowing how I feel about him.

'I think I can promise that for tonight at least,' she said.

'Good, so we are agreed that this night is to be out of this world.'

He was smiling now, a glittering, reckless smile, and she felt a thrill of something like fear, and yet she could not have turned back. For tonight, at least, Blake was to be hers.

CHAPTER EIGHT

IF this is a dream, let me go on dreaming, thought Gemma. From the moment they had driven up to the splendid entrance of the hotel and a chauffeur had taken the silver Mercedes away to park it, she had been happy in a way that she had never known before. She was content to be with Blake, to love every moment of the evening and to resolutely put at the back of her mind what was to happen tomorrow. The foyer was a glitter of crystal chandeliers suspended at a great height above the colourful Chinese carpet, its pastel pattern complemented by the blues and greens and pinks in the huge window above the curving staircase.

Drinks were served in a gold and blue room, the chairs of blue velvet intricately quilted and framed in gilded wood, and the tables were of some old Italian pattern also painted in gold. Blue velvet curtains hung from floor to ceiling with great swags of golden tassels supporting them. Quickly they were caught up into the party, given glasses of sparkling wine, that was exquisitely cold and refreshing. People greeted Blake and were introduced to Gemma, and she could tell by the way the men looked at her that they thought she was looking very attractive. Some of them even said so.

'What is it about you, Blake, that attracts the most beautiful girl in the room?'

'I couldn't say. You'd better ask Gemma.'

She felt his eyes looking quizzically at her. He probably thought it was a joke that this man should think she was in love with Blake. If only it had been a joke! She could feel Blake's hand possessively on her arm, and she wanted it to stay there. At least her appearance seemed to please him, for he probably thought she was doing him credit. After all, this was a business dinner, though one would hardly have thought so. It all seemed so gay and enjoyable, not in the least serious. Of course it was to promote various new kinds of wine and to meet people of the same profession. Blake seemed popular, but never once did he go away from her. She was surprised that he should be so attentive for she had not expected it.

'I'll be quite all right on my own, Blake, if you want to talk business with any of these men—or the women, of course. I don't mind if I'm left alone.'

Blake smiled.

'You wouldn't be left alone for very long looking as you do tonight, Gemma! No, this is our night, and I don't intend to let you forget it.'

All the business talk, whatever there was of it, seemed to take place before dinner. In the other room where the meal was to be served, the lights were subdued, small round discs in the ceiling giving an effect almost of moonlight, the only other illumination provided by candles. The seats were against the walls, golden-brown banquettes of buttoned velvet with high backs that gave privacy to each small table. Gemma had not expected to be so alone with Blake, but they were seated at one of the side tables and it was almost as if they were the only two in the room.

They could hear the hum of conversation coming from the other tables, the tinkle of women's laughter, the deep response of the men's voices, but it all seemed far away. The only thing that seemed real to Gemma was Blake's presence next to her on the soft velvet seat that was hidden from the next table by a division of wood padded with golden-brown leather. A small gleaming dance floor was in the centre of the room and music came from the dais where three musicians very softly played romantic melodies from another era. The haunting notes of the guitar seemed to set up an echo in Gemma's heart.

The wines were South African, but the menu for this important dinner was more the Nouvelle Cuisine of France than the more straightforward cookery of the Cape. There were globe artichokes, served with a lemon-flavoured vinaigrette, fish terrine, like pink marble, both beautiful and delicious in layers of white fish and pink shellfish with the occasional layer of fine chopped herbs and mushrooms. There were tiny venison chops cooked in juniper berries and served with a sauce of redcurrant jelly and bitter orange, and finally there was a gâteau de Pithiviers feuilleté, puff pastry light as air with a filling of almonds, sugar, eggs and cream. The courses were served slowly with plenty of time interspersed in which the guests danced or socialised as they wished.

Occasionally friends of Blake's discovered them as they were dancing, but, rather to Gemma's surprise, Blake did not encourage any suggestion that they should join the others. When they danced in the darkened room to Gemma it was as if they were alone, moving in some solitary dream that did not include anyone else. This was a different Blake from the one she had met and disliked the day when she arrived, a man who could easily charm if he wished and who seemed as if he wished to do so tonight. In the darkness he held her as if she were something infinitely fragile and precious, and when they sat together between dances, he touched her hand gently as if even this slight touch mattered and was of great importance to him this night.

On the shadowy dance floor, she was enclosed in his arms and she felt again the thrilling sensation that confused her whenever she was near to him and found herself thinking of the kisses she had had from that sensuous, mobile mouth, so very near to hers as he whispered, 'Lovely one, you really are the most beautiful girl in the room. Do you know that? Most beautiful and most alluring. Right at this moment, I could wish for a desert island somewhere a very long way from here, with no memories and no regrets. Just the two of us and this lovely, pliant body very close to mine.'

She was silent because she did not trust herself to speak. If she responded with some mocking reply, it would break the spell, and she did not want it to be broken. Not tonight, anyway. She would awake to reality soon enough tomorrow. But what about Trina?

she thought. Don't think of her. Blake is being charming to me.

'Is this some of that famous charisma?' she ventured to say, smiling up into his face that was so dark and finely featured against the dazzling white of his dress shirt.

'Of course,' he smiled. 'I do trust it's working overtime this evening, because I certainly intend it should.'

More coffee arrived in small gilded cups, together with a delicious apricot liqueur and chocolate truffles.

'I won't sleep tonight,' Gemma protested.

'What does it matter? Half the night has gone anyway. Sleep is for tomorrow. We'll find some place above the Indian Ocean to welcome in the dawn.'

And now they were in the Mercedes, coasting along the De Waal Drive, above the sleeping city where the lights shone, strung out in beads of silver and, in the harbour, trains still shunted, carrying goods to the lighted ships.

'Where are we going?' asked Gemma.

They seemed to be driving for ever into the darkness where, above in the cobalt sky, the Southern Cross shone in its splendour beside the streaming opalescence of the Milky Way.

'I promised we would see the dawn above the Indian Ocean, and we have to go quite a way for that,' said Blake. 'Here it rises over the mountains, but to see it come from the sea we must go as far as Simonstown. From there we'll see it rise from Cape Hangklip over False Bay.'

In Gemma's present mood, she did not mind if they had to go a hundred miles to see the sun rise. It would have been all the same to her. I'm happy, oh, so happy! she thought. I don't want this perfect night to end.

'Happy?' asked Blake as if he could read her thoughts, and she nodded as his hand touched hers.

He slid the car to a halt near Simonstown, just as the first streaks of rosy light were reflecting in the ocean from the eastern sky, and his arm enclosed her shoulders as he showed her the wakening landscape just as if he were creating it himself there in front of her eyes. A bright star and a crescent moon hung in the lapis lazuli of the morning sky and below this the rosy glow mingled with streaks of gilded yellow.

As the sun rose in dazzling rays of light stretching across the heavens, he turned her face to his and his mouth came down hard and firm upon her own. It was a long, long kiss and she did not want it to end. She felt content to let her emotions sweep her along in a passionate response that she had never known with any other man.

'Lovely Gemma, I think you'd better marry me.'

She was jerked awake from her dream. This was the last thing she had expected.

'What?' she gasped.

'Oh, I know I've always said I'm not the marrying kind, but circumstances alter cases. I desire you, Gemma—I want you. And you want me, if I can judge by your response to me. Maybe it isn't the grand love that both of us have known and thought we wanted, but you attract me quite strongly, and I, I believe, attract you. We've been two people lost in a maze. Let's both forget our pasts and build some kind of future out of the pieces. Perhaps neither of us believe in love any more, but there are other things beside love—physical attraction, for one thing, and you can't deny that we have something going for us in that direction.'

'I don't deny it,' said Gemma.

How can I deny it when his touch thrills me in this indefinable way? she thought—but he doesn't love me. He still loves Trina. So why is he proposing to me? It's unbelievable!

'What about Trina?' she asked.

Blake gave a harsh laugh.

'Don't worry about Trina. She's gone back to her husband. There was some slight hiccup in their marriage—all over now.'

'But why marriage to me?'

'Why not? You're a very attractive girl, and as I told Katy, I need to marry some time. You'll be most useful to me in the business. Oh, yes, I'm being very practical.

It's not just the glamour of the night that's weaving its spell on me. I've worked it all out.'

'I thought you wanted me to go,' said Gemma.

'What gave you that idea?'

'Something Trina said.'

'Oh, Trina—sometimes she has odd notions.'

So that disposes of that, she thought, or does it? No word of love, but at least he finds me attractive enough to want to marry me. But how can I? He's decided he needs to marry and has chosen me because I'm not unattractive and I could be useful to him in his business. Not very romantic, but oh, Gemma, the way you feel you have love enough for two.

'May I think about it?' she asked.

'Don't think about it. Answer me now while the magic of this night is still there. Answer me now. Say yes, you'll marry me as soon as possible.'

She looked at him in astonishment. He seemed so urgent and eager, and yet only a short time ago she had thought he was inextricably bound to Trina. Could she risk a marriage in which she was the one who loved the most? But if I don't, she thought, I'll regret it for ever. And if I do ... won't there be heartbreak there as well?

He was kissing her now and, with his kisses on her lips, all her resistance to the idea of marriage crumbled away.

'It seems like madness,' she murmured, 'but, Blake, I will marry you.'

'You promise?'

'I promise—but oh, Blake, if you decide tomorrow that it's all a mistake, tell me before it's too late.'

'Why should I decide it's a mistake, for heaven's sake? I'll get a special licence and we'll be married next week. Thank you, my lovely Gemma, you've taken a great load off my mind, and you won't regret it.'

She was so intoxicated by his kisses then that it was only when she was back in her small apartment making ready to sleep for a couple of hours that she remembered what he had said. Whatever had he meant? Why had he said, 'You've taken a great load off my mind'? Could his decision to marry her be to put him beyond the temptation of his involvement with Trina? She dismissed it from her thoughts that were in a kind of golden haze at the idea that soon, very soon, she was to become Blake's wife.

And it seemed it had not been a dream or a sudden impulse on Blake's part, to be instantly regretted in the cold light of day, nor had he followed up his astonishing proposal by passionate lovemaking as she had half expected he would.

'Sleep well,' he had said to her as he left her at the door of the Jonkershuis.

'But it's morning already,' she had protested. 'I must be at work in about three hours' time.'

'Nevertheless you need your sleep after last night. I'll leave a note for Piet to take over with Katy this morning and you can sleep for as long as you like. Meanwhile I'll set things in motion.'

He bent his head and gave her a kiss that was, surprisingly, as gentle as the flutter of the doves' feathered wings in the oak trees that were gilded now by the morning light.

Set things in motion? So he really meant what he had said. And did she herself mean it? Oh, yes, she told herself. Marriage to Blake is a quite terrifying prospect, and yet so blissful that I can't turn my back on it. I don't believe he loves me. He seems to think that Trina was the love of his life, but at least he must have some kind of liking for me, otherwise why should he have suggested we should marry?

She slept for a little while, but soon awakened again, too excited to sleep for long, and after she had showered and changed into a lilac flowered print dress with a flounce around the skirt and the neckline, she made her way to the main buildings. Piet was in the bar where the visitors had sampled their drinks and presumably Blake must by now be showing them around the wine cellars.

'Well, you are a dark horse, Gemma! Why did you never tell me that you and Blake had something going? I was convinced it was Trina who had him dancing to her tune, but it seems I was wrong. Congratulations, or

I suppose I should wish you happiness, shouldn't I? Congratulating the girl means you think she's pulled off some feat, doesn't it? And personally I think it's Blake who should be congratulated. He certainly has lots of sense to prefer you to that man-eater!'

Gemma hated his reference to Trina. She wanted to forget her. She looked at Piet's vivid blue eyes and wondered if she detected a slightly hurt look about their expression.

'It was some surprise,' he said now. 'I had rather hoped ... oh, well, let it pass. Maybe I wasn't too bright about things. I didn't think I should press you so soon after Dion's death, but it seems I was wrong. Of course I'm not stupid. I know I wouldn't have stood a chance against Blake. I can't blame you for going for him in a big way—all the girls do. At least,' he added hastily, 'they did. Not now, of course, not after next week.'

Next week? Blake must have even told Piet that he was planning to marry her next week. It seemed somehow to make it much more factual that someone else knew. Gemma went into the kitchen and all the girls crowded around her.

'Miss Gemma, we are so pleased! We all said you would be the one to marry the master.'

Then came Katy.

'What did I tell you? I knew I was right. You and the master were made for each other. God made you especially for him—that's what I told the master.'

I hope that impressed him, Gemma thought. She had no illusions that Blake was in love with her. Oh, yes, he found her physically attractive, but so were very many other girls. However, he had found that she was useful around his precious farm and he had decided it was the right time to marry. Was his decision tied up with Trina, the fact that she seemed lost to him now? Oh, Gemma, what are you doing? she thought in panic. It's not too late to pull out.

But when, later in the morning, he strode into the kitchen where she was working, her heart seemed to turn over.

'Come, Gemma, leave that. I want to speak to you for a moment.'

He's changed his mind, she thought, and was surprised by the extreme pain this thought aroused in her.

By now the visitors were arriving, strolling through the sunlit gardens where banks of blue hydrangeas foamed over the low stone walls like waves of the sea. Blake glanced at them irritably.

'All these people around—what a menace they are when I want the place to myself!'

Gemma laughed.

'You're glad enough to have them usually.'

'Not this morning. I need a little privacy today. Come to the stables, we won't be interrupted there.'

'But what about the visitors?'

'Piet and Katy can cope for a while. We'll join them later.'

He had her by the arm, hurrying her across the courtyard past the dovecote with its bevy of white fantailed pigeons preening and bowing on their ledges, past the great tubs of blue hydrangeas and amaryllis lilies. And then they were in the stables, in the cool whitewashed shade. The boxes were empty, as Koos had the white horses out and harnessed to the old Cape bus that they used to take visitors around the farm, and Jasper, the beautiful chestnut thoroughbred that only Blake could ride, was out to pasture.

'First this,' said Blake, and kissed her. Gemma knew then that whatever happened she loved him too much to deny him anything.

'Lovely one, do you remember that other day when we came here? Your eyes were big and blue and terrified. They look more beautiful now. When you look at me like that, Gemma, I could run away with you right this minute and make love to you all day.'

His hand cupped her breast, and her whole body seemed to be concentrated in that one place that swelled and hardened in delicious response to his touch.

'We can be married on Saturday,' Blake said. 'I've arranged it all as far as I can. That means we can go away over the weekend and be back for business as usual on Monday.'

He doesn't ask me what I think of the plan, thought Gemma, just takes it for granted that anything he says goes.

'How do you know I'm still of the same mind?' she asked him.

He laughed and his mouth claimed hers in a long kiss that seemed to penetrate to the very depths of her being.

'This is how I know,' he said. 'You want me as much as I want you—admit it.'

She shook her head, shaken and disturbed by the emotions that possessed her.

'You may try to deny it now, Gemma, but when we're married you'll find out that it's so. I'm going ahead with all the arrangements. The local church is sufficiently picturesque to show off that gown. We'll have the reception here. I've already phoned the caterers. I wouldn't expect you to arrange your own wedding feast.'

'But who will come?' asked Gemma. She had expected a quiet wedding with just the two of them at a register office.

'All my friends and acquaintances. You wouldn't expect me to marry in a hole-and-corner way, now would you?'

No, he would have to be flamboyant about it, she thought. Oh, Gemma, what are you doing? she asked herself. She could not imagine being Blake's wife, and yet she could not face life without him.

The next few days passed like some bright dream. Gemma felt she was being carried along in a fast-running current, being borne relentlessly farther and farther from the shores of her ordinary life. She had not realised how many friends Blake had. Somehow he had managed to obtain printed cards of invitation, and she sat for the whole of one evening writing out names that did not mean anything to her, strange names that seemed to have French or Dutch origin, but she noticed that he did not seem to have invited Trina, and for this she was thankful.

For these few days, Blake was strangely circumspect. If she had a meal with him, it was usually hasty and they were busy with some arrangements.

'I can wait,' he told her, 'but not for long.'

It seemed he was keeping away from her during the day too. She felt excited yet uneasy, as if she were rushing headlong into some course that might lead to her own destruction. Like Dion. Dion? How could she have forgotten about him so soon? And Blake seemed to have forgotten him too. But she had never loved Dion. She knew that now. She had never experienced such terrible emotions with Dion as now she did with Blake. Terrible yet ecstatic. And Blake? What did he feel? It was difficult to tell. Under that charming manner that he was using towards her now, she could still sense a will of steel. And she was still puzzled about his sudden determination to marry her, for, in spite of his assertion that she attracted him, he had never mentioned love.

At last came the morning of the wedding. Blake had insisted that the hairdresser and beautician should come to the house.

'You must have your hair done in the same way you had it before,' he told her.

'But surely I could do my face myself,' she protested.

'My bride must look beautiful, just as lovely as possible. I've taken so long to make up my mind to marry that now I want to show the world I've chosen well.'

'So I must look beautiful just for your friends, not for you,' she challenged him.

'For me too, of course. Everything I own must be beautiful, whether women or horses.'

'I'm glad you put the horses last,' she said ruefully. 'And I own myself at present, and expect to do so even after we're married.'

'Take care, Gemma. I'm a very possessive man. And after our wedding, you will belong to me, just as the farm does.'

She was to remember this later, but at the moment she had no sense of foreboding. Only some primitive emotion, old as time, sent a dark thrill through her body and she did not argue any more, although she had always considered herself a modern, liberated woman.

Blake was not to see her until she reached the church, but he arranged she should dress in the main house, saying the Jonkershuis was too small. So she had a beautiful room put at her disposal, with floor-length curtains of chintz in a design of roses, looped up with green banded swags, a bedcover of the same material, and an eighteenth-century dressing table in a kidney shape looped with fine lace and ribbons and with gilded candles held by winged cupids. Gemma could not help wondering whether this also showed some of Trina's decorative flair.

The Viennese hairdresser reached even higher standards in designing a hairstyle that had to suit the small pearl coronet holding the veil in place.

'You will look like a princess,' he promised her.

And when the last touches of make-up were applied and she stood in front of the long mirror, Gemma was inclined to agree with him. It was a pity she had worn the dress once before, but this time it looked entirely different, with its tight pearl-embroidered bodice over the flowing folds of the silk skirt. The bouquet trailed stephanotis from a spray of cream orchids. Everything was perfect. She thought of Blake's words when he had first seen the dress at the airport: 'Secondhand bride'. How little she had dreamed then that one day she would become his wife!

She was to be accompanied to the church by one of Blake's friends. She had not met him yet, but Blake had said he would call for her in his Rolls after Blake himself had departed. Katy was to come with them to arrange her train at the church door, as everything had been planned so hastily that there was no time to think of having an attendant. She came up to the room now to tell Gemma her escort had arrived.

'Oh, Miss Gemma, you look so beautiful,' she said. 'I'll want to cry. For certain I will when I see you in the church.'

'There's nothing to cry about, Katy,' Gemma assured her.

And yet there was. When she descended the stairs and saw the man who was standing in the hall, she had a shock. It was the same man who had brought her back to the house on that terrible day. How could Blake have done this to her? But he had probably forgotten. There had been so much confusion then that he would not have remembered such a thing. But the man, Miles, did.

'Well, this is a much happier occasion than last time when I met you,' he smiled. 'I do wish you every happiness. I must say Blake is a very lucky man.'

But what does he really think of me? she thought. He must think me very faithless to have forgotten Dion so soon, and again in her mind came the awful scene that had haunted her dreams for so long, the crashed car and Dion's poor maimed body. I'd put it to the back of my mind, she thought. Why has this man come to remind me of it on this particular day? But she tried to forget about this as they came to their destination.

The small church was built of rosy-coloured sandstone and had been there a long time, surrounded by tall trees and smooth green turf. Through the trees came a glimpse of the sea, azure blue with ships anchored far out in the bay, and sometimes the sails of yachts like large white birds. For Gemma, the service passed in a dream. Blake stood at her side making the responses in a firm deep voice, and she herself was surprised by the clear, bell-like sound of her own answers.

I'm right to do this, she thought. Whatever he feels about me, I know that I truly love him and I will do until death us do part. Then they were in the vestry being congratulated and signing the register, and next the organ swelled out its joyful sound as they walked between smiling people, strangers to Gemma but not to Blake. They are kind, she thought, they really wish us well, and she felt exhilarated and happy as she talked to the guests with Blake at her side. It seemed just like any other wedding of people who loved each other. And yet she still felt uneasy. If only he had ever said he loved me, she thought. He's so matter-of-fact about how useful I'll be to him in the business of the farm!

But he appeared pleased enough with her now. She had never seen him appear so elated before. Several people remarked upon it. 'You've done him a world of good, Gemma. I've never seen him looking so happy. What's the secret? How did you manage to charm such a confirmed bachelor?'

Soon she went away to change, as they were to go away and stay for the weekend in a friend's house at Plettenberg Bay. Blake had insisted that she was to buy a new outfit.

'If you don't have to buy a wedding dress, then you really must go to town on another dress,' he said, and she had bought a suit in palest gold silk that matched the topaz pendant and the gold bracelet that had been Blake's present to her on this day. Katy had offered her services, but when she had helped her off with her wedding dress, she sent her away, because she felt she must have a few minutes to herself after all the excitement and noise of the reception. She was sitting in her cream satin and lace underwear touching up her make-up when there was a knock at the door.

'Come in,' she called, thinking that Katy had come back for something, and she did not turn round.

Through the wide mirror she saw her, the one Blake had called the intruder on that night when she first arrived—Trina, dark and beautiful, her perfect tan set off by the bright flame-coloured dress that clung to every curve of her lovely body.

'Trina, what are you doing here?' demanded Gemma.

'That's a nice way to greet me, I must say! What should I be doing here? I came to congratulate the bride. Very remiss of Blake to forget my invitation, as after all I am one of his dearest friends. But perhaps you, Gemma, had something to do with that. You always did strike me as, shall we say, a wee bit jealous when I was here. But now I suppose you think you've won. Well, don't be too sure. I know Blake. He'd do anything to keep the farm.'

'What do you mean?' asked Gemma.

'You two have cooked up a pretty illusion of a romance, I must say, and all the guests seem most impressed with the charade. But we know, don't we, what the true story is? You look all sweetness and light, but wouldn't those guests be surprised if they knew you'd married with an eye to the main chance!'

'If you mean you think I'm marrying Blake for his money, you're very much mistaken. Blake asked me to marry him and I accepted, because I love him dearly.'

She hated herself for saying this to Trina. It had been forced out of her by the other woman's spiteful tone and the hatred in those flashing black eyes. Trina laughed mockingly.

'Don't give me that! I know the real reason for Blake's marriage. How much did he offer you to marry him before the final date?'

'I don't know what you're talking about. And now, Trina, I'd be glad if you'd leave me. I have to dress. Blake said I shouldn't take too long and keep the guests waiting.'

'And you must play the obedient little wife, of course. I wonder how long that will last. You must be pretty hardheaded to get over your fiancé's death so quickly and marry Blake just because he offers to pay you for it.'

'Look, Trina, you're quite wrong. Why on earth should Blake have to pay me for marrying him?'

'Oh, so you're pretending you're doing it for love, but I know that when I was here, he was so desperate that he was prepared to make an offer to anyone within reason who would marry him before the expiry date. He told me so.'

'What expiry date?' queried Gemma.

'You know very well what I mean. Don't play the innocent and try to pretend this is a lovely romance—it won't wash with me. You know as well as I do that Blake only married you because there was a clause in his uncle's will saying he had to marry within two years of inheriting the farm, otherwise it would go to a distant cousin.'

'What?' Gemma gasped.

'Of course you must have known,' sneered Trina. 'I guess his uncle made that condition because Blake was leading a pretty wild life at the time and he wanted him to settle down. Well, he has settled down, much more successfully than anyone could have believed possible. Blake tried to contest the clause, but it was no go. Of course when the will was made his uncle naturally thought that Blake would marry me.'

She paused for breath and for the first time seemed to notice Gemma's stricken expression. In the mirror, Gemma herself could see that she had become deathly pale under the make-up.

'You mean to say you didn't know? But how could that be? You must have noticed how worried and irritable he's been lately. We discussed his problem up and down when I was here and I agreed with him that there was nothing he could do except marry someone else, even if it was only a temporary measure. I could never have obtained a divorce in the time.'

'What am I to do?' Gemma murmured to herself.

'Do? What is there to do? Most marriages don't last very long these days, so what's the odds? When Blake has got legal possession of his farm, he'll be quite willing to buy you off, you can be sure. You won't suffer. And if you're fond of him, you wouldn't stand in his way, would you? Well, Gemma dear,' Trina walked to the door, 'I guess I've kept you long enough. Goodbye, my dear. Have a happy weekend—I'm sure you will with Blake. He knows how to make a woman feel a woman. I should know, but then I've known him for a long, long time. I'm not even jealous. I know it won't last long.'

CHAPTER NINE

GEMMA never knew how she got through the next hour. She sat at the mirror gazing at her own reflection and saying to that girl who had been so happy this morning, 'I should have known. Oh, God, what am I to do?'

It was Katy who aroused her from her stupor. She came bustling in, determined to carry the suitcases to the car and to help Gemma in anything she needed at the last minute. She was astounded when she saw that Gemma was still in her underwear.

'Miss Gemma, the master is waiting! Come, let me help you dress. *Ag, tog*, Miss Gemma, you are in a dream today, and no wonder!'

'Oh, Katy, I can't. I can't face all those people again!' Gemma said agitatedly.

'What is it now, my pretty one? *Ag*, shame, every girl feels shy on her wedding day—it's only natural. Come, let me dress you or the master will be coming to do it himself.' She laughed slyly. 'But that would take up too much time altogether, not so? He will get his turn later, isn't it?'

There's nothing to be done yet, Gemma thought, until we're alone. I can't make a scene in front of all the guests. Like a doll with wooden limbs, she let Katy help her into the beautiful gold silk dress and jacket, and the tiny tricorne hat with its plume of ostrich feather. Like some marionette, she stood at the head of the stairs that led to the patio and flung the bouquet to the assembled guests. She did not know or care who caught it. Then she was with Blake and felt his arm around her as everyone crowded forward, eager to bid them goodbye. The white horses, adorned with silver hearts and pulling a Cape cart, took them as far as the gate where the Mercedes awaited them. As they pulled away from the house, she turned back to wave at the crowd of guests and saw that a figure in a flame-coloured dress was holding the beautiful spray of stephanotis and orchids.

Following her gaze, Blake remarked, 'It was kind but rather unexpected that Trina travelled all that way to wish us well at our wedding.'

'Yes, I agree—it was rather unexpected. I noticed she didn't bring her husband with her,' Gemma added.

'I wouldn't have expected it. Her husband is a very busy man.'

'Too busy to keep his wife in order,' said Gemma bitterly.

'No, Gemma, surely that remark was uncalled for. Today's your wedding day. You should feel kind towards everyone. A bride should normally have charitable feelings towards the whole world.'

'But I'm not a normal bride, am I?'

'You're a very beautiful bride and, if it wasn't that I'm on a busy highway driving, I would show you in no uncertain terms just how beautiful you are.'

Gemma was silent.

'Are you tired, my dear?' asked Blake gently, 'Lean back and close your eyes. You need a rest after all the excitement.'

She closed her eyes, because she could not bear to look at him, to see those slim brown hands on the wheel and the clear-cut profile with the long curling lashes over the eyes of golden-green. However could she have thought she could be happy with this man? She had suspected he didn't love her, but she had not known he could deceive her in this way. He must have been desperate to ask her to marry him. All that mattered to him was that he should be able to keep the farm. In those circumstances, he would have married anyone who was reasonably presentable.

But how could he have made love to me like that if I didn't mean anything to him? she thought. But men are different. He finds me fairly attractive physically and I just happened to come at the right time. But what does he intend to do? Will he want a separation from me as soon as Trina can gain her freedom? Is that the idea behind all this? How could I have let myself get into such a muddle?

A friend of Blake's had lent them a house for the

weekend, a house, like a great white ship, aground upon its rocky pinnacle above the Indian Ocean. Every room had glorious views, some to the vast expanse of sea and the golden sands, and others inland to the blue mountains and forested slopes. There was a discreet bevy of servants, clad in spotless white and red turbans, and iced champagne awaited their arrival.

'Good to be alone at last,' said Blake, as he placed a long chair for Gemma on the glassed-in verandah that hung above the sea. 'This champagne you can enjoy. The other you hardly sipped.'

She accepted the drink, hoping it might give her courage. Blake was acting a part now, she thought, the role of the loving bridegroom, but it was difficult to resist the charm of that smile, difficult to believe that it was all an illusion and that he had married her with one simple desire in mind, to keep the farm on which he had expended so much effort and which, of course, he was completely unwilling to lose. He would pay any price for it, even the price of marriage to a woman he did not love.

Why could I not have continued in my dream? she thought. Oh, why did Trina have to shatter my illusions? And the temptation came to pretend, just as Blake was pretending. The wine seemed to create a golden haze in which she could not believe that he could have been so cruel in his deception.

'You're very solemn, Gemma. Aren't you going to drink to us?' asked Blake.

'I don't think it's necessary,' she said.

'That's true. We're going to be very happy without any nonsense of toasts,' he said. 'Oh, Gemma, you looked so absolutely beautiful today. When you came into the church, my heart skipped a beat.'

You're lying, she thought; you were thinking of how it would have been if it had been Trina.

The major-domo came in to announce that dinner was served.

'You're going to have a treat tonight,' Blake told her, 'Eugene's food is out of this world.'

They dined on langoustines, succulent and pink,

followed by partridges wrapped in bacon, small new potatoes and tiny green peas. Gemma ate what was put in front of her and it tasted like straw. Then at last they were alone in this beautiful house that was as modern as tomorrow.

The settee in the huge room overlooking the ocean was of marshmallow consistency. As she sank into it, she knew Blake would follow. And he did. At once she was in his arms and his kisses seemed to tear her apart. Almost she could have forgotten Trina had ever come between her and Blake with her revelation of his deception, but as he kissed her, the tears spilled over and she felt the taste of salt mingled with the sensuous softness of his lips on hers. He drew away from her, his mouth smiling.

'What's all this, then? Tears on your wedding night? You're very sweet, Gemma, astonishingly innocent in your reactions and yet so beautifully responsive to passion. Aren't I fortunate that I found you?'

'You are indeed, Blake.'

She got up from the settee, moving away from the overwhelming temptation of his embrace.

'There's no need to go on with the play-acting, Blake,' she said. 'Trina has told me everything.'

'What do you mean?'

'She's told me the reason you married me, that you needed to marry before the end of the month in order to keep the farm.'

The dark frown that clouded his face had hidden the charm of his smile.

'She was wrong to tell you that. I never intended you should know.'

'Obviously not. You say I'm innocent, but you must have thought me astonishingly naïve to accept your proposal of marriage, to believe that you were attracted to me after so short a time. It's really laughable! Anyone would have done.'

'Come, Gemma, that's simply not true,' he protested. 'You're a very desirable woman and you showed pretty clearly right from the start that you were attracted to me. I could easily have seduced you that time when we went to the Wild Coast, but I held back out of respect for Dion's memory.'

'You went out of your way to attract me because you needed to marry. But if you think you could have easily seduced me, you flatter yourself. Even if you had, it would have been better than this. How could you have made us stand in front of the priest making those solemn vows when all the time you only needed me for one purpose, to keep your precious farm?' she raged.

'Look, Gemma, be sensible. Perhaps I should have told you the reason behind my haste to marry, but it wasn't the only reason. And what would have happened if I had told you? Would you have accepted me under those circumstances?'

'No, of course I wouldn't!'

'So I thought. I did put it to you partly as a business proposition, didn't I? So why is it so much worse now that you've discovered an underlying reason? I've always been physically attracted to you. I never pretended there was a great love involved in the bargain.'

'No, you didn't, did you?'

They had been standing staring at each other like two angry cats, but now he strode towards her and seized her by the shoulders.

'But, Gemma, I can't see why you're so upset. It was a sensible decision to marry anyway, whether possession of the farm was involved or not.'

'Sensible?' exclaimed Gemma. 'Do most people marry for sensible reasons?'

Blake's touch, his nearness, the glowing sincerity of those long-lashed eyes, and the temptation of his lips so near to her own, confused her, softening her harsh hurt at his deception.

'Poor girl, was it romance you wanted? Do you still believe in fairy tales?'

'Not now,' Gemma told him.

'You seemed an ideal wife for me at this time in my life. I needed someone pretty desperately to conform with the stupid clause in my uncle's will, but it's not true that I would have married just anyone. You came along at the right time, and we do find each other physically attractive. You're a very beautiful woman and you will always do me credit both as a hostess to my friends and in my business. I'm pleased with my side of the bargain so far and expect to be better pleased later on. You will be too, I promise you.'

Gemma drew away from him. Away from his grasp, she was able to speak more steadily.

'I made no bargain. I didn't know there was any bargain being made.'

'Most marriages involve a bargain and an element of risk too. Why should this be any different? If you had married Dion, it's possible you would have made a worse choice.'

'Don't bring Dion into this!' she snapped.

'So that's it—you're having second thoughts! I hoped you'd forgotten Dion, but it seems you haven't.'

'That's beside the point. What matters is that I didn't know your real reason for this hasty marriage and, now I do, I want none of it!'

'Ah, but my dear Gemma, it's rather late to change your mind now. We're well and truly married. Didn't the priest tell us so?'

'There is such a thing as annulment. If I leave you now this night, it will be as if the marriage never took place.'

He came over to her and, seizing both her hands in his, slowly and relentlessly he drew her towards the settee.

'My dear Gemma, you'd never do that to me, would you? For me to keep the farm, the marriage has to be ratified in the only way a marriage can be. There can be no talk of annulment.'

'The farm, the farm! That's all you have in mind! But it's no good, Blake, I'm leaving you now. I can't go on with this.'

He was pushing her down on the settee, holding her with arms of steel.

'Those vows can't be broken. You can and will go on with this marriage. You're my wife now. Your vows can't be broken by some girlish whim.'

'How can you call it a girlish whim, that I'm shocked because you tricked me into marriage?'

'Hardly tricked,' he pointed out, 'You were eager to marry me, don't deny it, and soon I'll show you why you wanted it. You'll understand your desire when it's matched with mine, as it soon will be.' She was being held down by the weight of his body upon the soft cushions, like a fawn in the grasp of a leopard, and his gold-green eyes had the exultant expression of a conqueror. His long brown hands stroked her breasts, coaxing them into response, and his kisses demanded that her lips should open.

Somehow she tore herself away from him and ran swiftly towards the door that led on to an outside staircase, curving downwards past the rocky cliffs and on to the beach, far, far below. A huge moon had risen over the sea and shimmering paths of light made the scene silvery yet distinct. Gemma was only conscious of this passionate urge to get away. She could not clearly visualise what was to happen if she left Blake, but she knew that, if she stayed with him, she would be lost. The wind caught her as she opened the door and made to run down the white steps.

'Gemma come back—what are you doing?' she heard Blake's shout behind her, but, taking off her shoes with their high heels and delicate straps, she ran on, hearing his footsteps pounding behind her until she was on the silvery fine sand with the sea breaking in white-edged foamy waves and glittering cobalt blue beyond in the darkness.

It seemed like hours that she ran in the darkness, the wind in her hair, the fine sand crunching under her feet, but, on the edge of the sea, he caught up with her. She felt his arms holding her, chaining her to him until she gasped for breath.

'Little fool, crazy girl, what do you think you're up to? You can't escape from me so easily—and what's more, when this night is out, you won't want to!'

Gemma tried to struggle away from him, but his hands were like iron bands.

'I can't go on with this, Blake,' she gasped. 'You

must realise I have no intention of being married to you now that I know the reason you persuaded me.'

'And you didn't need much persuading, did you? Come on, Gemma, stop struggling. I'd hate to bruise that beautiful skin. You're my wife, maybe only in name at the moment but soon we'll change that, so no more talk of annulment. That just isn't in the programme, but this is.'

Easily and lightly he swung her into his arms and carried her back up the white moonlit steps.

'You wanted romance,' he said. 'Well, now you have it.'

His lips were bruising hers and all gentleness had gone.

'You didn't think I'd let you get away, did you? Beautiful, desirable Gemma, you must know I'm determined to have you. Tonight you will belong to me. That's been on the cards since I first set eyes on you. The fact that our marriage makes it possible for me to keep the farm takes second place. Forget it. Don't think of anything else but we two, and how beautiful it's going to be when you lie in my arms.'

I love him, she thought. In spite of everything, I love him. Can I forget that he had a cold calculating reason for marrying me? Can I forget that Trina spoke as if she owned him and was lending him to me for the shortest possible time?

His lips were warm upon her own, and his hands more and more demanding and she could feel that the whole of her, body and mind, wanted nothing else but to respond to his urgent lovemaking.

'No more running away,' he said, as he carried her into the next room where the huge bed was hung with curtains of turquoise silk. Here the sound of the waves was muffled into a soft singing like that of a convoluted shell placed beside the ear. She felt the long zip at the back of her dress sliding easily down under his long fingers and then his hands were on the smoothness of her back and the tiny clasp of the wisp of lace and satin upon her breasts was undone. As her garments were discarded, her body felt strangely soft and yielding in thrilling contrast to the hard masculinity of his own.

Even at this moment she thought she could detect a look of dark triumph upon his face. I've lost, she thought. I should have fled away when Trina came to see me. Now it's too late. I can't resist this overwhelming passion he can arouse in me, even though I know it will lead to nothing but heartbreak.

This then was love, she thought, this pain that was pleasure, this sharing of her body with another one that was strange and yet beloved, this ecstasy that led to an unknown place that was still breathtakingly familiar, a country of shimmering shafts of lightning that pierced the clouds and released their warm rain into her pulsating body.

When it was over, she lay with his dark head on the soft curve between breast and shoulder, hearing the distant sound of the sea beyond the shore, mingling with the beat of her heart. How relaxed he looked, how young, breathing so quietly in sleep beside her. It's as Katy said, we were made for each other, she thought, and yet a cold, small voice said inside her, he doesn't know that. He's made love to other women, but for me there's only been one man—Blake. Was it just as usual for him, and will he compare me with Trina and find me wanting? Plagued now by these restless thoughts, she at last fell into a troubled sleep.

The dream came again, the dream she had thought she had left behind her. She was watching the track and seeing again that streamlined monster hurtling round and round, taking Dion to his death. The car disintegrated into a hundred pieces of metal and Dion's body lay there, maimed and broken. This time she rushed on to the track and tried horribly to lift him. Then suddenly, frighteningly, he was alive again, speaking to her from a bleeding mouth, saying, 'Tonight I'll show you how to love.'

She heard herself screaming, 'No, no, Dion, not that! Dion, oh, Dion!' and burst into wild tears.

In her sleep she fought against the arms that were holding her.

'Let me go! Dion, oh, Dion!'

'Quiet, Gemma, quiet! You're with me. Don't you know where you are?'

Consciousness returned to her. Blake was holding her firmly against the hard muscles of his chest and she was aware that her face was wet with tears.

'Calm down, Gemma, stop fighting against me. Are you properly awake now?'

She gave a long shuddering sigh. It felt so good to have Blake beside her after that horrible dream.

'Yes, I'm awake, I think. I'm sorry, did I disturb you very much?'

'You did indeed. A joyful bridegroom hardly expects to be wakened by his bride calling to another man.'

He had turned on the light at the table by his side, and now he reached for her nightgown where the servants had placed it beside the bed.

'Put this on, Gemma.'

Obediently she reached out her arms to slip into the garment of chiffon and lace that was so fine, the shop assistant had assured her, it would pass through a wedding ring. She was still shuddering from the shock of the dream and yet Blake made no attempt to help her. Instead he left her side and put on a maroon silk gown that suited so well his dark good looks. His expression was bleak as he looked at her. Only a little while ago she had been naked in his arms, and yet now, as she shivered, in her lovely nightdress, she was painfully aware that it hardly covered her breasts. And he seemed to be aware of this too, because he handed her the matching long-sleeved, collared gown and said abruptly, 'Put this on too.'

The rapid beat of her heart, accelerated by the frightening emotions of her dream, slowed down now into painful heavy thuds. Blake's expression, so cold, so distant, terrified her.

'Do you often call to Dion in your sleep?' he asked.

Gemma shook her head, her fine red-gold hair cascading about her face.

'I don't know. I don't think so, Blake. I have this dream.'

'What dream?'

'He seems to be alive again, but this time it was more vivid than usual.'

'Because you wanted him instead of me, because you were feeling guilty that I made love to you.'

'No, Blake, no, it can't have been that. I was just restless.'

'And why were you restless, because you felt you were sleeping with the wrong man? A fine thing when on his wedding night a man has a ghost for his rival.'

'It isn't like that at all. You don't understand, Blake.'

'I understand enough to realise this whole thing has been an enormous mistake. You said you wanted none of the marriage now, but I was fool enough to think you didn't mean it, fool enough to think I could change things by making love to you.'

You did, Blake, you did, she wanted to say, but his cold grim expression held her back. How could you vow eternal love to a man who after all married you to get possession of his farm? And with this thought, her indignation returned.

'How can you be so righteously angry about my dreaming of another man, when all the time it's Trina you're thinking of? If Trina had been able to get a divorce in time, you would have married her, you can't deny it. You only married me because I was conveniently available, so how can you expect me to feel anything at all about you?'

His frown was dark and she felt a shudder of fear trickle coldly down her spine.

'Leave Trina out of this! You've always shown yourself madly jealous of her. But did our lovemaking mean nothing to you then, Gemma? Was it only a poor imitation of what you'd expected to have with Dion?'

'I didn't choose that you should make love to me,' she retorted. 'I suggested an annulment, but I still think leaving you would have been a better idea.'

And that's true, she thought. Whatever happens now, I'm heading for a broken heart.

'And you didn't enjoy being made love to?'

'No,' she lied. I won't betray my feelings to him, she thought.

'Well, you could have fooled me! However, Gemma, you need not fear my unwelcome attentions again. I can face up to most things, but I can't fight a ghost, that's for sure. In future you can sleep alone, alone with your memories—and may it make you happy!'

CHAPTER TEN

BACK at the farm, Gemma felt as if she were acting a part, the role of the happy bride. Blake is better at deceiving people than I, she thought bitterly. He's had more practice.

She slept in the large room that was the original chamber for a newly married couple, a room with an enormous four-poster bed, covered by an intricately worked white lace coverlet. The floors were of shining yellow-wood with jewel-bright strips of Persian rugs, and there were huge old armoires made of stinkwood that would have stored clothes for a multitude. In one corner of the room there was even an old cradle, intricately carved. Some expectant father must have spent many loving hours on this masterpiece, Gemma thought, and she wondered how many children it had held in all the years that the old house had stood. How firm marriages had been in those days, and how secure the brides of Bienvenue must have felt in this lovely room surrounded by all this beautiful solid furniture. They must have looked forward to a long happy life with their husbands and children in this beautiful valley of the Cape.

It was hurtful, the way Blake put up an elaborate pretence for the sake of the servants. He left his clothes carelessly draped around the room for them to deal with and the rather spartan bed in the adjoining dressing room, in which he slept, he made himself. To Gemma he was unfailingly courteous in front of company so that anyone would have thought they were a normal newly married pair. But, when they were alone, he was cold and distant. At night she lay wakeful in the wide bed, and thought of him sleeping on the narrow couch in the next room. Sometimes, when she woke, hearing the constant chorus of cicadas in the trees beside the house and the haunting call of a curlew far away in the farmlands, she would be seized with a desperate longing to open the other door and beg him for some affection. But no, she could not do that. Her whole soul shuddered away from the idea. She imagined the scorn on his face if she betrayed that she longed for his physical presence, ardently desired his lovemaking. But that's all over, she told herself. Somehow a barrier has arisen between us that it's impossible to cross, and anyhow, he never really loved me, only used me for his own purposes.

'Miss Gemma, you look too thin for a bride,' Katy told her. 'Married women should be nice and fat, not *skraal* like a bad milking cow!'

Very flattering, thought Gemma, and there were lavender shadows under the blue eyes that Blake had once admired.

Piet, nice simple Piet, seemed to sense that something was wrong. Gemma would not have thought he could be so perceptive. He came into the wine cellar one day where she was arranging the glasses for the next lot of customers.

'Hi, Gemma, you look paler than usual. Are you feeling a bit rough lately?'

'No, Piet, I'm quite all right—just a bit tired. You must remember I'm not used to this heat.'

'But you seemed to thrive on it at first. How come it doesn't suit you now?' A sudden thought seemed to occur to him and his face became more brick coloured than usual. 'You must forgive me—I didn't think of it. I'm a clumsy oaf!'

'If you mean I might be pregnant, Piet, the answer is no,' said Gemma quietly.

'I didn't mean . . . .' His confusion was painful.

'Piet, you're sweet to worry about me. I'm quite all right, really.'

'You don't look it,' said Piet. 'I hope Blake is looking after you properly. He's a grand chap, but I don't know that he understands much about women.'

Gemma laughed, and it seemed as if she had not laughed for a very long time. Piet smiled at her, not sure that he understood the joke but glad that he had produced this effect.

'Let me in on this, won't you?'

Blake was standing in the open doorway of the large winery. His eyes were dark with disapproval.

'Glad you can amuse my wife, Piet. I don't seem to be able to. Shouldn't you be supervising the bottling of that Late Harvest? I thought we discussed it yesterday.'

'Of course, Blake. I was just going.'

And with that Piet vanished in the direction of the other cellars, looking rather downcast.

'There was no need to be so unkind to Piet,' Gemma told Blake sharply.

'And there's no need to have him hanging around my wife!'

'It's a pleasant change to have someone hanging around, as you so gracefully put it, who's not scowling at me all the time,' she retorted.

'You always did seem to enjoy his company, didn't you? He was making a bit of a play for you before, wasn't he?'

'Before you did, you mean. Yes, I think he was.'

'Did the ghost of your former lover hold him off as well?'

'Certainly. He treated me with respect because of Dion, I think.'

'And I didn't. Well, I got my just deserts for that, don't you agree?'

'Anyhow, Dion was never my lover,' said Gemma. 'You should know that.'

'Yes, that's so, surprisingly enough in this day and age. What happened? Were you making sure of the wedding ring?'

'Oh, you're impossible, Blake!' she cried.

'Impossible, am I? And what about you?'

This was only one of many scenes that passed between them when they were alone, but, in front of other people, Blake acted the attentive husband. Gemma found herself caught up in a whirl of social activity, for it seemed as if Blake was determined they should spend as little time alone as possible. This was difficult for Gemma. Her proud spirit rebelled at having to accept clothes from a man who obviously despised her and she tried to manage with the few trousseau clothes she had brought with her, but Blake soon objected to this.

'My wife must dress in a suitable fashion,' he declared, and he opened accounts for her at the most expensive boutiques in Cape Town. 'Buy some good clothes,' he told her. 'You may as well look the part of the pampered bride, even if we know that our marriage was a failure from the start.'

'I can't run up accounts in your name,' she protested.

'Why not? It's yours too, isn't it? I thought you married me for a safe pay cheque.'

'Well, you certainly did, didn't you? That simple ceremony won you the farm, so perhaps after all I am entitled to use your name.'

In a fit of pique, Gemma went out and bought lovely and lavish clothes for every social occasion—fondant-coloured linens, for morning, striped delicate silks for evening, Italian shoes in fantastic shapes.

'How slender your figure is, madam,' the shop assistants flattered her. 'And what gorgeous hair! With your colouring, you could make anything look fabulous.'

She spent more on beauty care, visiting the hairdresser more frequently, experimenting with make-up. The woman she saw in her mirror was infinitely more sophisticated than the girl who had come from England with so much hope and so little experience. Something had happened to that soft, vulnerable mouth and the look of wide-eyed innocence, but, hidden beneath this perfectly groomed exterior, there was a hurt woman lacking love.

'We must give a party, quite a big affair, the first since our marriage,' Blake decided.

'I hadn't noticed anything to celebrate,' Gemma said coldly.

'Maybe not, but it will be good for business.'

'Well, of course, in that case we must give a party.'

Blake ignored her attempt at sarcasm. She glanced at

him and thought it was a long time since he had tried to charm her with his smile and his persuasive ways. It gave her a pain at the heart when she saw him using that charisma on the tourists, seeing the way he gave them that easy smile that didn't mean anything. I have no attraction for him any more, she thought; now that he's got his desire to keep the farm, he's no longer interested in me—if he ever was. It was all a play acted with one purpose in mind, and now he's achieved the object, he doesn't have to pretend any more.

And where does that leave me? How long does he intend to keep up this farce of a marriage? Just until Trina can become free? I must face up to the fact that I no longer mean anything to him, if indeed I ever did, and I must go away somewhere, however anxious he is that I should stay for the sake of appearances. But if I leave here, I may never see him again. And, in spite of everything, my heart can still miss a beat when I see him appear, smiling and laughing with his parties of tourists, but never smiling at me.

Soon I must confront him, she thought, find out what he really intends—but not just yet.

Meanwhile the days went by, days of golden summer with the grapes ripening on the vines and the song of the workers harmonising in the vineyards that stretched in green leafy rows up the slopes of the hillsides. They were hoeing the weeds, but soon it would be time to pluck the sun-drenched grapes, and then the leaves would turn yellow and blow away in the wintry winds and rain of the Cape that could be so mellow with its sunshine but sometimes savage in its storms.

The Christmas season was approaching, and it seemed strange to Gemma that this festival was to take place in a land drenched in sunshine, although the shops were full of seasonal reminders, artificial snow and many a perspiring Santa Claus distributing presents to children with bare feet and sun-dresses.

It was all go for the party which was to take place on Christmas Eve. Blake demanded perfection, and although he employed caterers, it involved quite a lot of work for Gemma, and added to this was the fact that this was the height of the tourist season and she was particularly busy in the day-to-day catering for the visitors.

'Buy yourself some splendid outfit,' he commanded. 'I certainly never want to see that wedding dress again.'

'And neither do I,' she told him. 'It doesn't hold many happy memories for me, you may be sure.'

But it did—bitter-sweet memories of that night when he had charmed her into consenting to marriage, memories of the little church and the look on his face when she met him at the altar. Now it was all like a dream. And even then he had been acting a part.

By now the summer heat was tremendous and, for the party, Gemma chose a dress of palest green silk organza, its bodice a fragile knotted arrangement over her breasts, its skirt in fine pleats that showed a shadowy glimpse of tanned legs, her feet clad in bronze sandals with high heels and one slender strap. Her hair, lightened by the sun to a paler gold, was drawn away from her face in an intricate coil. The style emphasised the fragility of her face, the way the high cheekbones had become a little too evident during the last few weeks.

Blake, she thought, as she came down the stairs and saw him in the reception hall, had put on his party face already, for he even smiled. Above dark trousers, he wore a white mess jacket as a concession to the heat, and a maroon tie.

'You're looking very beautiful, Gemma,' he said.

'Thank you.'

She felt her cheeks glow pink under the careful make-up as she saw his eyes inspecting her appearance slowly and consideringly. It seemed to her the first time he had properly looked at her since their wedding night. Something flashed in the sombre darkness of his eyes and then was gone.

They stood together to receive their guests and Gemma was painfully conscious of his presence there beside her. As he easily presented some friend she had not met before, the touch of his hand on her bare shoulder could still thrill her as no other man's touch had ever done before.

Afterwards she moved around among the guests like a woman in a dream. She must, she thought, be playing the part of the happy bride, because people she met talked and laughed with her as if she charmed them, but every now and again she felt Blake's eyes on her and she wondered whether he was approving of her in her role of hostess to this crowd of strangers.

The beautiful house this night seemed to have come into its own. The wide double front doors were flung open on to the patio and the whole length of the inner hall that extended from front to back was revealed in all its glory with its shining yellow-wood floors and beautifully carved old furniture. The soft lights of the chandeliers shone flatteringly upon the women's pastel dresses and creamy shoulders, and the men's white jackets contrasted startlingly with their bronzed faces.

'A glorious evening, a really beautiful start to the Christmas season,' Gemma heard on all sides.

But it will be a bleak Christmas for me, she thought. Suddenly, for the first time since she had arrived, she had a wave of homesickness. She thought of her sister, complete with new baby and husband, in the cold midwinter of England's climate, enjoying a quiet family Christmas so many thousands of miles away from here, and she wondered whatever she was doing in these luxurious surroundings, lapped in comfort but deprived of kindness and love.

'You look unhappy, Gemma—is there anything I can do?'

It was Piet, looking unaccustomedly smart in his bright blue tuxedo that contrasted with the blondness of his hair and his ruddy fair colouring.

'No, no, Piet. Everything seems to be going well, doesn't it?'

'Yes, it's a lovely party. Blake really is an ace at arranging these affairs, isn't he?'

'I suppose he is,' she agreed.

'It was a good idea having it start early, because most people like to go to church to the midnight service on Christmas Eve.'

'Yes, I was hoping . . . oh, well, we'll see.'

No use, she thought, thinking sentimentally that there might be a reconciliation of sorts if they went to church together. They were too far apart.

She looked towards the door, where Blake seemed to be greeting a latecomer. His tall figure hid whoever it was and she made towards them, knowing he would expect her to do her duty by the new guest. But she felt Piet's hand on her arm as if to check her.

'I didn't know you'd invited that woman,' he said.

'Nor did I,' Gemma replied.

She saw two slender hands with long scarlet nails resting on Blake's shoulders and, as the two figures turned, there was Trina, dark and exotic against the background of light panelled wood. Unlike the other women, who wore floating dresses in pastel colours, she had a bright coral-coloured dress of silk jersey, encrusted with glittering silver bugle beads. At the back it plunged to well below the waist and was held at the neck in halter fashion by a thin mandarin collar. At her hips, emphasising their curves, was a scarf of Aztec design lavishly tasselled with silk. Her dark shining hair fell away from her head in a kind of ordered confusion of rippling curls.

Then Blake was turning and calling across the crowd.

'Gemma, see who's here.'

'I must go,' Gemma said to Piet.

She moved slowly towards the pair of them. Why had Trina come? Had Blake been in touch with her since their marriage? Of course he must have been; that was only to be expected. She saw with a pain at her heart that Blake had his arm around Trina's beautiful bare waist. Indeed Trina was keeping it there, her hand on his.

'Oh, Gemma,' she said now, smiling brilliantly, 'we're back again in town for Christmas, and when I heard you were having a party, I simply had to come to bring my greetings to you both.'

'And your husband? Is he not with you?' asked Gemma.

'Unfortunately not. He had other business. I came myself in my small hired car, though I was just telling

Blake it gave me trouble on the way here. That's why I'm late.'

'Well, now you're here, you must have something to eat and drink,' said Blake.

'Nothing to eat, darling, just a little champagne, and do you think Shadrac could serve it on the little side patio where there's that swinging seat? That way we could get away from the crush and it would remind me of old times. You wouldn't mind, Gemma dear, would you? I particularly need to speak to Blake on his own.'

'Feel free,' said Gemma, and called Shadrac to order the champagne.

She was furious both with Trina and with Blake. How could they both humiliate me in front of all the guests? she thought. Blake must have asked Trina to come and he never told me. Does that mean that he's been meeting her in secret?

She made her way around among the guests, trying to chat in a carefree fashion, replenishing glasses, bringing people together.

'Where's Blake?' one woman asked her.

'Oh, somewhere around. He had some business he wanted to discuss with Trina.'

'His business with Trina should have been over when he married you, my dear. Don't be too trusting, will you? Oh, forgive me, I shouldn't have said that. It must be all this delicious wine talking!'

At last they came in from the patio, Trina with shining eyes, her hair deliciously ruffled.

'Forgive me, Gemma, but we had so much to talk about. You do understand, don't you?'

'No,' said Gemma coldly. 'Should I?'

Trina laughed with a tinkling sound of icicles breaking.

'Your wife can be very amusing, Blake!'

'I haven't found it so,' Blake replied, frowning.

By now the guests were beginning to depart, each one wanting to thank their hosts and give them greetings for Christmas. To Gemma it seemed never-ending, as she stood beside Blake exchanging polite and meaningless pleasantries with the crowd of guests. She seemed to sense that Blake was more affable than usual. Could that be because of his time spent with Trina? Gemma despised herself for the vivid jealousy she felt at the thought of the two of them together, but she could not help it. Had they discussed her and did Trina know the true state of their marriage? If she did, she would feel nothing but pleasure that the marriage had broken down before it had even begun properly.

At last most of the guests had left, but still Trina lingered, a flame-coloured figure in the background, chatting animatedly now to Piet. At last she turned to Blake and Gemma.

'Gemma, would you mind awfully if I borrowed Blake for a few minutes? My little car gave me so much trouble on the way here, and I would welcome his advice before I go.'

'Certainly, Trina. I'd hate you to be delayed, but why not take Piet along with you too?'

'Oh, no, Gemma, I'll leave Piet with you. I don't want to monopolise all your men.'

She took Blake by the arm and they left in the direction of the parking ground, where Blake had arranged an array of flaming torches to light the way.

This cool exchange had not been lost on Piet.

'I shouldn't get worked up about her if I were you, Gemma,' he said. 'You're twice as beautiful and ten times more attractive than Trina, and in any case, you've got Blake, haven't you? He preferred you to her. So why worry?'

'Oh, Piet, you're very sweet, but you know only the half of it.'

The strain of the evening and the sudden appearance of Trina had unbalanced Gemma. Normally she kept a tight rein on herself, but now her voice trembled and she was close to tears.

'The whole thing is a mess, Piet. I should never have come here, never have married Blake.'

'Nonsense, you don't know what you're saying. Look, Gemma, this night has been wonderful, but you're worn out. Why don't you go to bed and leave me to clear up things? The servants have done most of it already. Don't take any notice of Trina—she's known Blake for a long time, but you're the one he married. You're the one he loves.'

'You couldn't be more wrong, Piet,' said Gemma.

She wiped a tear away with the back of her hand, hoping Piet wouldn't notice, but he put his arm around her and she hid her head against his shoulder, ashamed of displaying so much emotion to him.

'What's all this, then? Oh, Gemma, don't do this—I can't bear to see a woman cry.'

'I'm sorry, Piet.'

His arms came around her and for a few moments she leaned against him, feeling his soft kisses on her brow as he tried in his clumsy way to give her comfort.

'Sorry to break this up, Gemma. What gave rise to this touching scene, I wonder?'

Blake stood there, his expression dark and furious.

'I came to tell you I have to take Trina back. Her car has broken down.'

'Oh, Blake, surely she could get a lift with one of the other guests!' groaned Gemma.

'She wouldn't want to do that. Besides, most of them have gone already. I must take her. I hardly think I'll be missed here. Piet seems to be looking after you well—too well, perhaps.'

'As you say,' said Gemma. 'How long will it take you? When do you expect to be back?'

'Quite a while. Don't wait up for me. But why do you ask?' His suspicious gaze rested on Gemma and then on Piet.

'I had thought we intended to go to the Midnight Service together,' she told him.

'Sorry about that. Can't be helped.'

'Piet is going,' she said. 'I think I'll go with him.'

'I don't think that's a very good idea.'

Muttering something about not keeping Trina waiting, Blake made for the door.

'I don't think you should come with me, Gemma,' said Piet awkwardly. 'Blake looked angry when you suggested it.'

'I don't care how he looked. If he can go with Trina,

I'm free to come with you. How dare he object to our going to a church service together?'

Piet shook his head.

'I don't understand it, Gemma. I thought you and Blake were the ideal couple. Why let a woman like Trina get in your hair? I'm certain she doesn't mean a thing to Blake any more.'

You're wrong, Piet. It's I who don't mean a thing, Gemma said to herself, but she did not say it out loud. She was sorry for Piet, caught in the backlash of Blake's anger against herself, but she was determined to defy Blake. How dared he almost forbid her to go with Piet when he was going to spend the next couple of hours or longer with Trina, who every time she saw him made a dead set at him, regardless of the fact that she already had a husband?

In defiant mood, she set off with Piet, but when she arrived at the little red stone church, she felt she was punishing herself. It was the church where she and Blake had been married so short a time ago, and, kneeling there, hearing the music and smelling the fragrance of lilies, she felt such anguish that she wondered whether she was going to faint. But becoming aware of Piet's anxious glance, she pulled herself together and gradually the calm majesty of the Christmas service took over from her thoughts. She came out in a more peaceful state of mind, and yet immediately she was plunged into explanations about Blake's absence when she met again some of the friends who had attended her party.

'He was so sorry not to come. He had to take a guest home,' she explained, and thought she surprised one or two knowing looks among them.

She heard the echoing cries of 'Have a Happy Christmas,' as they found their way to Piet's car. What a hope! she thought. It wouldn't surprise me if Blake had decided to spend Christmas with Trina. But no, they were expected at a large buffet lunch with one of Blake's farming friends. Would Trina be there too?

She dreaded getting back to the house and finding it

empty, going up to that large lonely room that had brought joy to many former brides but not to her.

'Let's go somewhere for a drive, Piet,' she suggested. 'I don't want to go home yet.'

'I don't think we should.'

'Please, Piet, just for a little while. Blake won't even miss me—he's too involved with Trina this evening.'

'You know I'd do anything for you, Gemma, but Blake's going to be pretty mad with you if you're late. He wasn't that keen on your coming to church with me.'

'Let Blake be mad!' she snapped. 'I don't really care what he feels. Besides, he won't be there. I can't go home and brood all night knowing that he's with Trina.'

Piet sighed as if he didn't know how to deal with her in her present mood and said, 'Very well then, would you like to go up Signal Hill? From there we can see the lights of Cape Town.'

'Anywhere so long as it isn't where Blake is,' said Gemma.

It was almost the same route as she had taken with Dion that ill-fated day before his death, but this time Piet was at her side, driving slowly and carefully around the precipitous curves of the road, upwards towards the great face of the mountain that towered above the city. It was floodlit tonight and its wrinkled surface looked like the skin of an aged elephant.

At last they were at the top of the lookout under Table Mountain, the place called Signal Hill. Piet parked the car and they walked towards the edge. Below them the lights of the great city were strung in their regular rows like strings of diamonds. Christmas illuminations shone in bright reds and greens, and sounds of music floated upwards from the city with cries of revellers showing there were many people still wakeful and out of doors on this warm Christmas night.

There were other people up here too, cars parked with lovers embracing oblivious of others, and there were shadowy figures holding each other close as they contemplated the wide view below them. I'm a stranger here too, thought Gemma, and in spite of Piet's presence, she felt weighed down with loneliness.

'What is it, Gemma?' asked Piet. 'What's troubling you?'

'I can't tell you, Piet. Don't ask me.'

'If it's Trina who's bothering you, I don't think it's worth worrying about her. She'll be back in Johannesburg in a few days, you'll see. I'm quite sure you're the only one for Blake now.'

'You don't know why he married me,' she said bitterly.

'I know how I would have felt if I'd married you, and I'm sure Blake feels the same. He married you because you're the most attractive girl around here and the sweetest and the bravest. Trina can't hold a candle to you. Oh, Gemma, if I were your husband, I certainly wouldn't be attracted to a woman like Trina. I'd know when I was well off.'

'I think we'd better go, Piet.'

The conversation, Gemma felt, was getting too dangerous. It had not been fair to Piet to let him bring her to this place, with its atmosphere of romance and the sensuous emotions created by the lovers around them. This is no place for me, she thought.

'You can't help knowing how I feel about you, Gemma,' he sighed. 'Blake senses it too, unfortunately.'

'Don't say any more, Piet,' she begged. 'Don't let there be anything between us that we could regret.'

'There won't be, but always remember that if you need me, I'm there, even if it's to have a shoulder to cry on.'

He started the car and, mostly in silence, they drove back to the farm. The place was still blazing with lights.

'Shall I come in with you?' Piet asked Gemma.

'Better not. I'll be all right on my own.'

There was no sound as she let herself into the house, except for the loud ticking of the longcase clock in the hallway. The servants had cleared up the remains of the party because they wanted to have tomorrow to themselves, and it was as if this evening's reception had never taken place. It was strange and rather frightening to meet such silence after the previous noise and chatter of the crowd. Gemma turned off the lights on the little fir tree in the corner of the room, and after she had dealt with the other switches, she walked slowly up the stairs to her room. Of course Blake had not returned. She hadn't expected it. He must still be with Trina.

She made her way along the shining corridor with its polished kists and pieces of Delft pottery on brackets, its old Persian runners, and, turning the brass handle of the heavy door into her own room, she let herself in. Here there was only one lamp lit, the one beside the bed, and the rest of the room was in darkness. A small armchair stood near to the fireplace, its back to the door, but as Gemma entered, it was swivelled around to face her. Blake sat there, his powerful frame filling the small chair to capacity. He was dressed in his scarlet robe, and this seemed to emphasise the darkness of his hair and the frowning expression of his face.

'So,' he said, his eyes seeming to take in every detail of her appearance, 'you're back at last. May I enquire where you've been until this hour?'

'You know where I've been, Blake. I told you I was going to church.'

'With Piet, and I said I would prefer you not to go.'

'I would have preferred that you didn't take Trina home, but you did so.'

'Really, Gemma, Trina's an old friend. I've told you before that you must stop this ridiculous dislike of her. When has she done you any harm? She always tried to help you in every way when she was here before. And tonight she came specially to be at your party when she might have gone to any other one of her friends.'

'Very good of her,' said Gemma.

'Let's leave your unreasonable prejudice against Trina and discuss your attachment to Piet, shall we?'

'My attachment to Piet? Really, Blake, this is ridiculous!'

'Ridiculous, is it? And where, may I ask, have you been with Piet since the church service? To my knowledge it must have been over at least two hours ago.'

'I didn't want to come home. I asked Piet to take me for a drive and he took me to Signal Hill to look over the city.'

'Signal Hill? You should know by now that that's a place where lovers go. And what else did you do besides looking over the city?'

'Really, Blake, you're quite wrong if you think I have any interest in Piet. He's a terribly kind, nice fellow, but. . . .'

'Don't give me that, Gemma! Before and after our marriage, Piet has been making a play for you. It's quite obvious that he's in love with you. Can you deny it?'

'I ... no, I can't deny it. Maybe he has some mistaken idea that he's fond of me. How can I help it if he is?'

'You admit he's in love with you and you encourage him by going to a noted parking spot for lovers at two o'clock in the morning, and yet you say you're not interested in him! Your faithfulness to the memory of Dion doesn't seem to affect your relationship with Piet,' sneered Blake.

'I tell you I have no relationship with Piet—and you can leave Dion out of this!'

'That's rich! How can I leave him out when he's spoiled our marriage?'

'What was there to spoil?' demanded Gemma. 'You married me because you wanted to save the farm for yourself—you admitted that. And now it seems that every time you see Trina, you regret it.'

'That's absurd! Trina has nothing to do with the present situation, which is that you used me for a substitute for Dion when we were first married and now you seem to have fallen in love with Piet.'

'I have not fallen in love with Piet! Oh, Blake, you won't or can't see. . . .'

'What won't I see?'

That I'm in love with only one man, she thought, but he's not in love with me.

Something in her expression must have penetrated his cold, rigid front, for he strode over to her and now his hands were on her bare shoulders and his gold-green eyes were gazing searchingly into hers.

'Oh, God, Gemma, those innocent blue eyes! If I thought that any wife of mine had even looked at another man, I'd. . . .'

She tried to keep cool, although his grasp on her shoulders seemed to set her whole body on fire.

'Really, Blake, this is madness! How can you talk of me as I were really your wife? Our marriage has been a falsehood from beginning to end!'

'But it hasn't ended yet, Gemma. If you can give yourself to Piet so easily, you can give yourself to me too. Forget Dion. Forget Piet. Tonight you'll know what it is to have a real lover, not just the memory of one!'

Now his hands were pushing down the slender straps, loosening the soft folds of her dress until it fell in a flurry of pleats at her feet and she stood naked before him. The silk of his gown fell open and he quickly discarded it as he carried her to the bed.

He took her angrily and with wayward passion, and yet, though at first she struggled against him, at the last Gemma responded to him against her will, knowing that she loved him and fearing that he might never again make love to her like this.

CHAPTER ELEVEN

GEMMA awoke from a deep dreamless sleep feeling wonderfully at peace with herself. She turned, expecting, hoping to see Blake beside her, but the room was empty. Why had he not stayed until she wakened? In spite of everything was he still angry with her? She got up, put on her gown and went into the dressing room, but that was as usual, the bed neat and made up. Now she went to the window and looked out on to the stone patio and the long driveway with the tall oaks on either side, gilded by sunlight. It was a glorious morning. Over the patio, the ancient vine that had been there almost as long as the house dripped grapes like green jewels, clustered tightly together, and deep blue hydrangeas spilled over from the containers cut from wine casks, banded with copper. Some way down the drive, a fountain, in a pool with white surround, splashed out its cool spray from the conch of a cherub in the centre.

This morning the sound of sweeping which usually woke her was absent and she remembered that, of course, it was Christmas Day and the servants had been given the time off after last night's hectic festivities.

So where was Blake? The joyous feeling she had had when she first awoke began to evaporate. If last night had been a new beginning, as she had hoped, his absence was a strange way to show it. She remembered that they were due at a buffet lunch at noon and it was now going on for ten. Blake had mentioned it would take them an hour to get there. After her shower, Gemma chose a dress of brightly striped silk, turquoise and light tan on a cream background, and a strappy pair of sandals in matching colours. She drew her hair back in a tortoiseshell clasp, as the day promised to be hot.

Downstairs there was coffee bubbling on the stove, croissants heating in the oven, but no sign of Blake.

Honey, the spaniel, was whining at the door, and when Gemma opened it, shot off like a rocket, scattering the doves that were pecking on the stone courtyard. Gemma set a table in the shade of the vine, putting two delicate wrought iron white chairs beside it. On impulse, the other day, she had purchased a Swedish ornament of gilt angels that rotated at the turn of a switch, and now she put this as a centrepiece and watched it processing slowly around. She poured herself a cup of coffee and sipped it, seeing the white pigeons from the dovecote bowing and hopping together in a seemingly endless dance of love, and she began to be oppressed by the quietness, for this morning she seemed to be the only person left in the world. Even the usual clamour of the servants, their loud voices calling cheery greetings to each other, was missing.

Then Honey set up a whimpering again and in a few seconds Gemma heard it too, the sound of horse's hoofs pounding upon the gravel of the drive. Blake came in sight, seated on his favourite Jasper, the black stallion that only he could ride. He was clad only in a pair of blue jeans, and as he came nearer, Gemma could see that both horse and rider were damp with exertion. In front of the patio, he slid to the ground. She looked carefully at his face, longing for some sign of the tenderness she felt for him, but she was met by an expression so indefinable that she could not hazard a guess at his thoughts.

'Good morning, Gemma. I see you found the coffee. A cup would be very welcome right now, but I must go and rub down the horse first and it looks as if I need a shower myself. Don't wait breakfast for me, I can manage to eat a croissant on my own.'

She felt dismissed, and later, sitting beside him in the silver Mercedes on their way to the lunch, she found his manner cool, even forbidding. Did he regret what had passed between them last night? Did he feel he should have kept faith with Trina? Or was it that he had taken her in anger and now repented of it? Could it be that he was still angry with her over her drive with Piet, who had not put in an appearance today because he was to spend it with his family?

There was little time for reflection when they arrived at the beautiful farm in the Paarl valley. This too was an old house from the time of the French Huguenot settlement, but it had never been neglected like Bienvenue nor had to be restored. Its pergola in front of the house was supported by square ridged white pillars dripping with mauve wisteria and the impressive gable above the doorway was scrolled in baroque style. All around the entire farm there was a white wall known as a *ringmuur*, and this had originally been built to keep out the wild animals that roamed the Cape in the early days of settlement. The farm was in a most lovely setting, a gem of a building against a backdrop of high blue mountains, with rocky crags at their summit.

The tall trees surrounding the house made a dappling of shade on the green lawns, and guests wandered around there, sipping their iced fruit cup and chatting amiably to each other. Others splashed in the round swimming pool beside the house that was a concession to modern ways. Sylvia, the hostess, slender with creamy olive skin and dark straight hair held back in a bun at the nape of her neck, seized upon Gemma and took her around, introducing her to very many of the guests until she felt too bewildered to remember any names. When she was finally allowed to come to rest and sit with a group of people, who were sipping drinks upon the old paved stoep, she looked across and saw that Blake was with Trina. Of course she was here. Gemma had been half expecting this, but she had not thought that she and Blake would be talking together as if no one else existed in the world.

'Don't you agree, Mrs Winfield?'

'I'm sorry, I missed that,' she said now as she tried to follow the conversation going on around her. These people must think her dreadfully rude that she had been so inattentive.

'We were discussing whether there's as much romance in this day and age as there was in the past when this house was first built.'

'It depends what you mean by romance,' said one woman. 'In those days, people married for life. Even if you married at sixteen, you stuck to the same man whatever happened. Now people feel free to chop and change. Maybe they have more romances that way—I don't know. What do you think, Gemma?'

'I think, when you've found the man you truly love, it would be good to believe it could last for a lifetime,' said Gemma.

'There speaks the newlywed!' someone said. 'But in this day and age, that's rather an impossible ideal, I'm afraid.'

'Maybe it is,' agreed Gemma.

She was watching Blake and Trina wandering away together into the walled garden that was hidden from view to the rest of the buildings. Trina's possessive hand was on Blake's arm and she was looking up at him with her dark eyes. Gemma could imagine the alluring expression of them. She had seen it before. How could Blake go back so swiftly to be under Trina's spell after what had passed between him and Gemma last night? Or had it meant nothing to him? Had it been a sudden impulse of passion brought on by his anger with her and Piet? And now he seemed to be avoiding her. But when lunch was served, he came back to her, meticulously polite, enquiring whether she wanted wine.

'Is there anything else you want?' he asked.

She smiled ironically.

'Only that you should keep away from Trina.'

'Trina's only here for one day. She'll be gone tomorrow. She needed some advice.'

About what? Gemma wondered. About when to get a divorce?

This Christmas lunch was very splendid, with cold meats and the traditional turkey as well as all the varied fish dishes of the Cape and, to follow, great halves of watermelon scooped out and filled with exotic fruits, papaya, grenadilla, peaches, apricots, early grapes and strawberries. A sparkling wine, ice cold, was served in long slender glasses and iced coffee was there for those who did not want wine.

Afterwards in the heat of the afternoon only a few energetic people sought the tennis courts and the swimming pool. The rest found the shade and lay on long chairs, in a semi-comatose state, it seemed. Blake had been roped in for a game of some kind and Gemma found herself alone again. She wandered over to the walled garden feeling that she would like to be by herself away from the crowd. It was a delightful place, a cool retreat from the heat of the afternoon sun, a garden with espaliered peach trees, green willows fountaining over a small pool, and sudden scents of honeysuckle, jasmine and roses. She sat on a stone seat, listening to the splash of a small fountain and seeing the bright iridescent green flash of a malachite sunbird seeking honey with its long curved beak in the depths of a flower. Then, all at once, her peace was shattered.

'Ah, there you are! Sylvia told me she'd seen you coming this way, so I came after you. I think there are matters we should discuss, Gemma.'

Trina sat down beside her, taking off the large sun-hat she had been wearing. She wore a sun-dress of vivid emerald green and her shoulders were glossy, bare and brown. Her luxuriant hair sprang away from her head in dark rippling waves that seemed to shimmer in the heat. Even after a morning spent in the sun, her make-up was perfect, her lips glossy and red and her lashes thickly curling above brown-shadowed eyes.

'What matters are those, Trina? I thought you'd done all the discussing you wanted to do with me the day Blake and I were married.'

'Yes, I certainly set the cat among the pigeons there, didn't I?'

Gemma thought that Trina herself looked very like a cat now, her confident smile tilting her small mouth, her eyes a little slanted in a smooth feline way.

'Blake was mad at me for telling you about the will,' said Trina. 'He hadn't intended you should know. He's so generous in some ways, you know, and he hates a woman to get hurt.'

'I hadn't noticed that,' said Gemma.

'You're still feeling sore at me for telling you, aren't

you? But truly I was sure you must know. I didn't realise you thought Blake was marrying you just for the sake of those beautiful blue eyes. I made sure he'd offered you money to do it. Anyhow, I'm sure he'll see you come out all right from all this. He's very grateful to you for saving the farm for him, I'm sure.'

'Yes, I suppose he is,' said Gemma. Though he doesn't particularly show it, she thought.

'You must understand it was so very important to him that he had to do something desperate about it.'

'You call marrying me something desperate?'

'Well, he had to marry someone, didn't he?' Trina shrugged. 'Just think what he had to lose.'

Gemma stood up.

'Trina, I think we've discussed all this quite sufficiently now. If there's nothing else you have to say, could we consider the conversation closed?'

'Oh, but I haven't come to the most important part, Gemma. I was trying to lead up to it tactfully.'

'You could have fooled me,' said Gemma.

In spite of her wish to appear unmoved in front of the other woman, her heart began to beat quickly. Trina had been the bearer of bad news before. What was she about to disclose now?

'I've been telling Blake the good news and I feel I must let you in on it too, though it's not yet public property,' said Trina.

'What good news?' asked Gemma.

She was quite sure it would not be good news for her.

'My husband has at last consented to give me a divorce, so quite soon I'll be free. Isn't that wonderful?'

'How would I know? I've never met your husband.'

'Oh, he's a dear and most terribly rich, but very, very boring, poor man. And I do so hate Johannesburg. It will be marvellous to live in dear old Cape Town again. Needless to say, Blake is delighted.'

'He is?' said Gemma drily.

'Naturally he was the first person to know. Oh, Gemma, I'm so grateful to you for holding the fort!'

'Holding the fort?'

'Oh, you must know what I mean. If it hadn't been

for you, Blake would have lost his inheritance. Of course, he'll see that you're properly compensated when the time comes.'

'The time comes for what?'

'Why, for your separation, of course.'

'You're suggesting I should leave Blake?' asked Gemma.

'Well, yes, knowing the circumstances of your marriage and why Blake had to do it, you would never stand in the way of our happiness, would you?'

'You seem to have forgotten one little thing, Trina,' Gemma pointed out. 'Getting a divorce takes quite a long time.'

'Oh, I'm not worried about that. Once my divorce is on its way, I'm quite willing to live with Blake until his own affairs are settled. People don't worry so much about these things half as much as they used to do, and after all, Blake and I understand each other. We've known each other for a very long time. Poor Blake, he never got over my marrying someone else, but now everything has come right again.'

But not for me, thought Gemma. Her impulse was to fight this woman and all her bland confidence that she was going to get Blake for her own. But what was the use? Blake had certainly shown in many ways that he didn't love Gemma. The moments of passion they had shared had not meant the same to him as they had to her, and Trina had been his first love and still seemed to hold some strong magnetism for him.

'I would suggest that you go back quite soon to the U.K. and forget the whole thing,' Trina was saying now. 'Poor Gemma, it's all been most unfortunate for you, but you won't come out of this penniless, I can promise you that.'

'Thank you very much,' said Gemma.

'Don't say anything to Blake about all this. He doesn't want you to know yet, but I was sure you would take it well. After all, it's only been a marriage of convenience, hasn't it?'

'Yes, I suppose it has,' Gemma agreed flatly.

'I thought you'd like to know about all this so you

can begin to think about making your own arrangements. Of course, Blake will provide your fare back to Britain.'

With that, Trina got up and moved away. Gemma watched her curving hips swinging sensuously as she made her way down the path to the beautifully wrought iron gate that shut the walled garden from the rest of the estate. Lunch had been very late and now it was almost evening, and pearl-breasted swallows were swooping and diving after insects in the still warm air. They had come from England, she thought, flying down Africa, venturing here against terrible odds. From another part of the garden, she heard the cry of a peacock, harsh and disturbing like a soul pleading for help. Trina's right, I suppose, she thought. There's no place for me here. I should never have come. It was all a great mistake, and like the swallows, I must go back, but unlike them, I can never return to this place.

Rejoining the crowd of guests, who were having a last glass of wine before departing, Gemma was surprised to find Blake at his most charming. He smiled and offered her a glass of wine as if she were the most important woman in his life. Perhaps she was, she thought bitterly, because it was up to her to consent to this separation. Trina was nowhere to be seen and Gemma concluded she must have departed, having poisoned her day.

Blake seemed so kind, asking her if she needed her stole now the evening breeze had arisen, looking at her as if she really meant something to him, but she supposed this was his usual play-acting for the benefit of the company. And was he especially happy because of Trina's news? Was this why he seemed so charming to her? He continued to talk to her easily and with charm even on the drive home, but the nicer he became to her the more she mistrusted his motives.

'You've had a long day, Gemma, and you seem rather pale and tired. What say I rustle up an omelette for us? I hardly think we need very much to eat after today's feasting.'

'I don't think I want anything to eat, thank you, Blake.'

'You must have something, and afterwards I have something very particular to discuss with you.'

Here it comes, thought Gemma. He wants to tell me about Trina. He doesn't know she's told me already. He wants to ask me to consent to a separation, and I can't face it. I don't feel I can take any more today.

'Oh, Blake, whatever it is, it must wait until tomorrow. I ... I have a splitting headache. I really must go upstairs. Please excuse me.'

With that she hurried away, and when she reached her room, she did something she had never done before and turned the key in the lock. Going over to the other door, she locked the dressing room as well. Then she discarded her clothes, had a shower and lay on the bed. Only this morning she had awakened to a kind of joy, but now that was all over and she tried not to remember her passionate response to Blake's lovemaking of last night, for she felt ashamed and bitterly humiliated when she thought of it. She should have realised that she was just a substitute for Trina and that, if he could get Trina, he would discard Gemma as quickly as he had married her. He had said she herself had used him as a substitute for Dion. That simply was not true, but she could never tell him now.

She heard Blake's footsteps along the passage, and then the handle of the door turned.

'Gemma, what is this? I've brought you some coffee. Open the door, for heaven's sake!'

'You can leave it outside, Blake,' she called.

'I certainly will not! Open the door! All I want is to give you some coffee. I haven't come to rape you—though after last night you probably think otherwise.'

'I'd prefer that you left it outside, Blake.'

'Look, Gemma, I don't think much of this idea. Open the door!'

'No, Blake, I want to be alone.'

Gemma felt she could not face hearing his explanation about Trina's coming divorce. She would have to hear it some time, she supposed, but not tonight.

'Very well, then, I'll leave you alone if you're determined to be obstinate. I'm not prepared to break the door down. Don't bother to lock the other door. If you really wish it this way, I'll sleep as far away from you as possible. I'll speak to you tomorrow.'

She heard a clatter of cups as he set the tray down and then his footsteps receding along the passage.

I've gained a few hours, but tomorrow I'll have to face up to the fact that I have to lose him, she thought. But how can I go on here, living in this house, seeing him every day until the time comes when he decides we must separate? I can't even endure the idea of seeing him tomorrow.

She sat for a long time brooding about her conversation with Trina, then the thought came to her suddenly, why shouldn't I leave now? I have my salary from all the time I've been here and which I scarcely ever had to use, and I have the little car that Blake gave me for my own use. I can return it to him later, but tonight I can use it to get away. If I leave him it will be far better than being dismissed like a servant, because I haven't proved satisfactory.

She threw a few clothes into a nylon pack bag, dressed in denim jeans and a cotton shirt, and cautiously opened the door of her room. Not a sound. Blake must be sleeping in another part of the house as he had said he would. She crept slowly down the stairs, afraid she might disturb the dogs, but Blake must have locked them in the kitchen tonight. Quietly she let herself out. She had brought a torch that lit her way to the stables where the cars were garaged, quite a distance from the house. Then she put the little car into neutral and pushed it out of the garage and as far as the driveway that sloped downwards to the road. Getting in, she let it freewheel until she was well away from the house, and only then did she press the starter button. Driving along the road to Cape Town, it dawned on her that she had not got a clue as to where she could stay or what she could do. She had no single friend who was not connected in some way with Blake, no one to ask if she could stay there while she decided on a course of action. I can always find some hotel, she thought. But can I go there in the middle of the night? She felt reluctant to face some curious night porter at this hour. I'll drive around until it gets light, she decided.

At this hour, the streets were silent and deserted, and Gemma found herself afraid to park in the great empty spaces of the city. She was drawn instinctively towards the place where there was light and activity and noise, the Cape Town docks where ships were being loaded regardless of the hour, and leaving her car, she wandered along the quayside, avoiding the shunting trains, and the cranes with their heavy loads swinging into space. As she walked slowly along, one or two men accosted her, obviously thinking the worst of a female alone at this hour, but, encountering her blank, blue stare, they went on their way.

Eventually, feeling utterly exhausted, she turned into a small café that was evidently open twenty-four hours of the day for its green-shaded lights were still lit and a middle-aged man was wiping down coffee spills on the plastic tablecloths.

'Are you open for customers?' asked Gemma.

'Sure, come right in, love. What can I do for you?'

His navy and white striped butcher's apron covered a large stomach and he appeared to have three chins, but his smile was as generous as his girth and his blue eyes below sprouting eyebrows looked kindly.

'Have you any coffee?'

'Certainly. And what are you doing here at this time of night, my girl?'

Gemma chose to ignore his question. The coffee, when it came, was better than she had expected, and she sipped the hot brew gratefully.

'Are you here to meet someone off a ship?' asked the man persistently.

'No.'

'Have you got some business here, then?'

'No.'

'There are safer places than the Cape Town docks at night for a young lady like you,' he said.

'I'll be all right,' Gemma told him. 'When does it start to get light?'

'Not for two hours yet. Is there something wrong? Have you quarrelled with your folks?'

Gemma had taken off her wedding ring and the man was evidently deceived by her youthful appearance into thinking she was younger than she actually was.

'I haven't got any folks,' she said now.

'Have you been turned out of your digs, then?'

'Sort of.'

He looked at her doubtfully.

'You don't look the type to be in any kind of trouble. But you never know these days, do you?'

'I'm quite a respectable character, if that's what you mean,' she assured him.

Gemma was getting a bit tired of the man's curiosity, but she was sure he only meant it kindly.

'Are you needing a job?'

Gemma looked at him, surprised.

'I suppose I am,' she said.

I can't go on living on Blake's money, she thought. It's true I'll have to find some kind of work.

'The woman who works here helping me with the cooking and serving had to go home because her husband's ill. I've had a hell of a time over Christmas, I can tell you, and now there's New Year coming up. It won't be for ever, but I badly need a temp until she can come back. Do you know anything about cooking? Just plain grilling and frying, of course. Would you be interested?'

Gemma looked around. The café was clean and simple, but it wasn't the kind of place where Blake would ever dream of looking for her. She could go to ground here while he and Trina sorted out their affairs. If he wanted a separation surely he could bring against her the fact of her desertion. Some day she would have to face him again, but this would give her a breathing space.

'I might be interested,' she said, 'but I have to find some place to stay.'

'No problem,' he told her. 'There's a vacant room over the shop if you don't mind roughing it a bit.'

She looked at him doubtfully. Was it too risky to

accept this stranger's offer? Working for him was one thing, but sleeping in might lead to complications, certainly. He must have read her thoughts by her expression.

'Look, girly, my name's Tom True, and I always tell everyone, True by name and true by nature. There won't be any funny business, you can believe me. My wife that I've had for twenty-five years would have something to say about that! I've got a daughter about like you, so you can rest assured I'll be straight with you.'

'Thank you, Mr True. My name's Gemma Maitland and I'd like to try your job for a while,' she told him. 'I think I could manage it.'

'That's settled, then, and you can call me Tom—none of this Mr True. Lock your door at night and you'll be all right here. I stay on duty until all hours and there's another chap who helps me out as well, but you needn't worry about him. He's pushing eighty, an old Navy man. He won't give you any trouble. I can vouch for him.'

And so it started. It was such an utterly different life she was leading that it seemed she was in a new country. Certainly she was kept busy, up at dawn with the strings of lights still climbing the mountain slopes, seeing the first shafts of sunlight gild the great ships in the harbour, then the smell of coffee, hot rolls, bacon, frying eggs as the workmen and sailors came in for a meal. She had a coloured woman for an assistant, who kept the place clean, but she herself was responsible for most of the cooking until Tom came to lend a hand in the evening.

She took the car to a garage and asked that it should be returned to Bienvenue, because she was afraid she could be traced through the car and she did not want this to happen yet. Would Blake be trying to find her, she wondered, or would he take her word for it that she wanted to disappear for a while? In the note she had written before she left, she had begged him not to look for her. She wondered, however, whether she should get in touch with Piet, but she could not risk it, although she was longing for news of Blake.

She felt as if she were living in a vacuum, marking time until she should hear in some way that Blake and Trina were together again. Then she would really consider going back to England, but not just yet, she told herself. She could not bear the idea of putting ten thousand miles between Blake and herself, even if he loved someone else and had never loved her.

CHAPTER TWELVE

IN this vacuum Gemma led her solitary life. She seemed to have developed some kind of immunity to the attentions of the sailors that she met in her café, and when she walked along the quayside admiring the great bulk carriers and the smaller shabby cargo boats that plied along the coast, she parried the remarks of the men with a friendly enough remark but a cool blue stare. She avoided the yacht club in case she should meet friends of Blake's who might recognise her, but sometimes from her little café she would see their sails like great white birds beating against the tide.

Tom True was a goodnatured man, and at this time in her life, after the harrowing emotions of the last weeks, Gemma felt even a kind of security in this job, although she knew it could not last for long. Sure enough, one day Tom announced, 'I had a letter this morning. Mrs Harris is due back next week. Her husband has recovered and she's able to work once more. So I'm afraid it's goodbye, Gemma. I'd very much like to keep you on, you've done wonders while you've been here, but I can't let Mrs Harris down—she needs the job badly. Her husband is never too well at the best of times. I'd like to keep both of you, but you can see how it is. I run the business with very little profit margin and these days everything costs so much, I just can't afford an extra hand.'

'It's quite all right, Tom. I knew it was only temporary.'

'What will you do? You haven't seen anything of your family since you've been here, have you?'

'I'll manage,' Gemma told him.

She chose to ignore his remark about her family. She had told him she had none, but evidently he didn't believe her. She could not help wondering whether Blake had made enquiries about her, or had he just accepted the fact that she had left? Was he glad of it? Did he think she would come running back as soon as she ran into any trouble? And what was she to do now? She supposed she should start looking for another job in a café, but anywhere else she would have to look for accommodation, and that would be costly.

Friday was always a busy day. Many of the workmen got paid then and came in able to afford the huge pieces of T-bone steak that had to be cooked on the large infra-red grill. Fishermen came in too, and sailors in port for the weekend. This evening, Gemma noticed a party of yachtsmen. It was unusual to get customers of this kind, but they must be seeking a change from the Yacht Club dining room. Well, fortunately she had never met any of them before. She was always afraid she might one day see someone from her life with Blake. But, as she served their steak and lingered around the table seeing to the wine that they had brought in themselves, she was startled to hear Blake's name mentioned.

'Careful, girly!' one of the men warned as the bottle bumped against the glass and a few drops spilled over.

'I'm so sorry—I'll bring you another glass.'

But she was listening to the conversation going on on the other side of the table.

'Yes, he's in the race tomorrow. He's had a long break after that injury. I wonder how he'll shape.'

The other man shook his head.

'Risky. But then Blake never minds taking risks. He was a superb driver up until a few months ago, but he hasn't had much practice since. I would have thought he should start on a low key instead of plunging in and taking on a major race.'

'The death of his assistant must have shaken him. I wonder he has the nerve to race again.'

'Oh, he's not lacking in nerve. I understand his wife was the other chap's girl-friend. They didn't lose much time, did they?'

'No, but I heard she's left him.'

'Really? Why would she do that?'

'Maybe she didn't like being married to a tough egg like Blake. There's another woman hanging around already, I hear—an old girl-friend. Trust old Blake, some people have all the luck!'

When the rush was over and things had quietened down, Tom was sitting with a glass of beer, scanning the newspaper for winners.

'Is that the sports page, Tom?' asked Gemma. 'May I have a look?'

'You can have it for keeps for all I care. None of my horses came in.'

Yes, here it was, under Racing. He even had a headline: 'Blake Winfield to try his luck again', and underneath this it described the car he was to use, apparently more hotted up than his previous one with even newer modifications. Oh, no, thought Gemma, not Blake! I can't go through that nightmare again.

'Would you be able to manage without me tomorrow?' she asked Tom.

'It's Saturday—you know that's our busiest time. You wouldn't want to let me down, Gemma? You never have before.'

'I'm sorry, Tom, but it really is something very important.'

'Oh, well, if you have to go you have to go, I suppose,' he sighed. 'I'll get Maggie to hold the fort, give her extra pay.'

Maggie was the girl who helped Gemma during the day.

'You can dock it from mine, but I'll try to be back by evening,' Gemma promised.

'Don't rush,' said Tom. 'I'll expect you when I see you.'

'Do you mind if I use your phone?'

'Feel free.'

She had decided that she must phone Piet. It was time she broke her silence. She had been too long without news of Blake and now this! She felt horrified that he should be going back to racing. What was Trina doing, she thought, not to be able to dissuade him from it? Fortunately she managed to get Piet at her first attempt. She heard his gruff voice with a feeling of relief and felt very close to tears.

'Gemma—good grief, where are you, girl? Blake's going to be over the moon when I tell him you've phoned! He's not at the house tonight. I guess he's over at the track doing a last tuning to the car.'

'Oh, Piet, that's what I phoned about. Blake mustn't know. I don't want him to know I'm here.'

'Where's here? And why don't you want Blake to know? You've had us all worried out of our minds not knowing where you are!'

'You might have worried, Piet, but I hardly think Blake has,' Gemma said sadly.

'He's tried all ways to find you and he's acted like a sulky bear since the day you left.'

'Maybe he has, but that's just because he needs to know where I am for his own benefit. Oh, Piet, what's he doing racing again? I thought Dion's death had cured him for ever.'

'It had, but your leaving him seemed to make him reckless again.'

'I don't believe that, Piet. But he knows I hate racing. Perhaps he's doing it just to show me how little he cares.'

'No, Gemma, that can't be true. I don't understand it about you two. I had thought you were ideally suited and very much in love—and now this! Really, Gemma, you're a fool to take so much notice of a woman like Trina. She should go back where she came from, and good riddance!'

'Well, she doesn't, does she? No, Piet, it's over between us, but I can't let him start racing again without trying to stop him. Will you take me to the race track tomorrow?'

'Willingly, but of one thing I'm sure, Gemma, even you can't dissuade Blake from going in this race. He's set his heart on going in to it. You'll never persuade him otherwise. In a way it seems he thinks of it as a vindication of Dion's death. He seems as if he's doing it to revenge that.'

Next morning, Gemma dressed in culottes and shirt of blue and pink fine stripes with a scarf to match worn on her head as a bandeau. Tom was suitably impressed by her appearance. He was so used to seeing her in working clothes, he hadn't apparently realised she could look so elegant.

'Whoever you're going to meet, he's going to like it,' he told her.

She had arranged to see Piet at the entrance of the docks and it was good to see him waiting for her there, broad and brown, his rugged shoulders bulging in his safari suit. She embraced and kissed him, and he held her tight for a few moments.

'*Ag*, Gemma, why did you do this to us? The old place isn't the same without you. Katy and all the girls are missing you so, and you dare hardly speak to Blake these days!'

'I think he'll be happier without me, Piet,' she said.

'I don't believe it. You two are as obstinate as each other. You should have stayed with Blake to save him from Trina. It's she who's put him up to racing again, I'm sure of it.'

'Trina? How could she?'

'Oh, she likes to be seen with the rich and famous. She likes to see Blake's name in the papers and for people to make a fuss of him. Never mind that he really should be paying attention to the farm instead of spending all his spare time at the race track.'

'Is that what he's been doing?'

'Of course. He's even closed the tourist side of the business. He's still paying the staff and he says it's temporary, but who knows? It was so popular too.'

When Gemma arrived at the race track she felt terrible, as she had known she would. She tried to banish from her mind the memory of Dion and the shattered car, but it kept coming back to her over and over again.

'Take me to Blake,' she asked Piet. 'I want to get this over with.'

'You look very pale,' he said worriedly, 'Are you all right? Wouldn't it be better to see him after the race? That way you wouldn't upset each other so much.'

'No, Piet, I must see him now.'

He led her to a place where the drivers put on their gear, and went inside. In a little while, he came out looking grim.

'He's not too pleased that I've brought you here, but he says he'll see you.'

'Very good of him,' said Gemma coldly.

'Now don't be like that, Gemma, and don't upset him before the race. I'll leave you to it.'

In the tiny dressing room allotted to drivers, Blake looked taller and bigger than Gemma's memory of him, but his face, she thought, looked drawn and thin, the features more aquiline, emphasising that arrogant expression. His regard was unsmiling.

'So you've come back at last. Nice to have another man tell me he's found my wife for me.'

'No, Blake, I haven't come back—you needn't be afraid of that. When I left it was for good. We only need meet in the future to arrange about a separation.'

'But why did you go so suddenly and with no explanation?'

'I just felt that night that I couldn't take any more. I had to leave. I couldn't bear to see you again.'

'I understand. You've made it pretty clear how you feel about me. As we both concluded from the start, the whole sorry business has been a mistake.'

'If you say so. Anyhow, it's all over now. Too late for tears. But, Blake, it isn't too late for one thing. If you have the slightest regard for me at all, you'll give up this crazy idea of racing today.'

His green eyes looked directly into hers. Gemma thought how cold they looked, like still tarns on a mountain top.

'I can't do that,' he said.

'You must know how I feel about it now. Please, Blake, don't race today!' she begged.

'How does it concern you, Gemma? You've left me anyway, haven't you?'

'I still don't want you to come to any harm.'

I still love you, she wanted to say.

Blake smiled wryly.

'Good of you, but I'm not intending to come to any harm. I drive safely. I'm not Dion, as you seem to have shown me on more than one occasion.'

'Oh, you're beastly to turn that against me! How

could I help the dreams I had?'

'Maybe you couldn't, but it showed me what way the wind blew, didn't it? How could our marriage succeed with Dion for company?'

'How could it succeed with Trina haunting us?'

'You have an obsession about Trina,' Blake said coldly.

'I thought it was you who had that. Anyhow, even without Trina, I can't see how you expected me to put up with the fact that you married me in order to secure the farm.'

'Look, Gemma, this isn't the time or the place to start mutual recriminations. I have to be at the starter grid in ten minutes.'

Gemma felt desperate. All she had succeeded in doing was to have an unpleasant scene with Blake, and she had meant to be so tactful, to plead with him and persuade him that she could not stand the fact of him going into the race. And, as usual, she seemed to have botched the whole thing.

'Blake, I'll do anything you want if you'll only give up the race. I'll go away and never come back again, never see you again.'

'Anything? Very generous of you, Gemma, but you've practically done that already, haven't you? And oh, by the way, don't worry about your ticket to the U.K. I'll arrange it whenever you want to go. Trina said you didn't intend to stay here. And now, Gemma, I really must be going.'

Suddenly he put his arms around her and, to her utter astonishment, kissed her long and hard.

'This is me, Blake, kissing you, not Dion, not Piet—remember that. Goodbye, Gemma. Enjoy the race. You always have liked Piet's company better than mine, haven't you?'

He was gone, and she felt utterly defeated. She had not succeeded in dissuading him from the race, only made things worse, possibly. She hoped she had not ruined his concentration. She had been told that nothing must interfere with that in the time before the race. Now she felt that she had done wrong to come here. Her lips felt bruised. Oh, how was it that he could still make her feel like this even if he sounded as if he had come to hate her?

Piet was waiting for her at a discreet distance from the place.

'Did you see Blake?' she asked.

'Yes, what did you do to him? He went past me looking as if the hounds of heaven were after him.'

'Oh, Piet, I don't want him to be in this race!' she said desperately.

'Are you sure you want to watch it? It's the first one, isn't it, since . . . ?'

'Yes, it is. But I'd feel worse if I didn't watch.'

From their seat on the stand, Gemma could see the pits and it looked exactly like the scene she remembered from that other day when she had only just arrived, the same blonde girls hanging around, the drivers in their weird crash gear, bulky, scarcely human, and the cars being nursed by the careful, swift hands of the mechanics, but looking like vehicles from another planet. She could see Blake's dark head as he talked and laughed with the mechanics. Trina did not appear to be there; perhaps she was already seated on the stand.

Then the drivers were putting on their crash helmets and taking their seats at the grid. She saw Blake's car was blue and silver, almost the same as the one that Dion had driven. Oh, surely she could have been spared that! I can't bear it, she thought, but I'll have to.

'Wouldn't you like me to take you back, Gemma?' asked Piet.

'No, I'll have to go through with watching it now,' she told him.

And then the flag went down and there was the noise again, the sound that had haunted her dreams, the high scream of racing cars at full throttle. This was her nightmare, a multitude of cars rushing round and round the track, seemingly never-ending.

'He'll be all right,' Piet tried to reassure her. 'It's safe as houses with him.'

Blake was winning. With each lap he pulled steadily ahead. This was different. There was none of that wild driving that had horrified the crowd when Dion drove.

The speed was fantastic and yet you felt the driver was in full control of the monster, not being hurtled around by something he couldn't handle.

'There you are, you see,' said Piet. 'I told you you needn't worry about Blake. He knows what he's doing.'

Gemma relaxed a little. Perhaps it was foolish to feel so dreadful about the race. Thousands of people were watching it and apparently enjoying it too. Why couldn't she be like them? Dion's accident had been brought on by his own foolishness. Blake was strong and careful. Nothing would happen to him.

But she had reckoned without the hazards of other drivers' folly. There was one man there who seemed to take particular risks, a man in a black car and black helmet, looking, to Gemma's overheated imagination, like a messenger of death itself. She had noticed him on each lap trying desperately to catch up to Blake, seeming to almost nudge the car as he tried to make Blake give way. Several times he almost got through, but Blake was determined he shouldn't. He used evasive tactics, leaving the other driver little room for manoeuvre. On the corners he stuck to his line. But at last the man, becoming frustrated by his lack of success, came too near to Blake's car and the two vehicles scraped each other, touching along the sides.

It was Blake's car that suffered. The crowd screamed as it swerved, momentarily out of control. Blake tried desperately to right it, but one wheel went onto the grass at the side of the track and the vehicle, losing traction, spun around facing in the opposite direction, spun back again and crashed into the barrier.

Gemma saw Blake's body slumped over the wheel. He did not move. She saw the marshals rushing over to the car and struggling with the seatbelt, and she knew that any moment the great car might go up in flames. The nightmare was with her now, real and actual, not in a dream. She felt Piet's arms around her, holding her in her seat.

'Let me go!' she cried. 'I've got to go to him!'

'You can't run across the track. Wait, Gemma!

There's nothing we can do to help. They'll do everything possible.'

'But I must know. He's dead isn't he? Blake's dead, and I never told him how much I love him!'

'The ambulance is coming. We can go down now, Gemma.'

Piet found a way through the crowd. She heard him saying, 'I have his wife here.' How strange—that's me, she thought. And then she was being helped into the ambulance.

'He's unconscious,' she heard the attendant say. 'We can't know how badly hurt he is until we get there.'

Blake's hand felt cold as they sped through the city streets to that hospital below the mountain.

'Oh, Blake, please live! I love you,' Gemma said to him, not caring that the ambulance aide was looking at her with pity in his eyes. 'I love you, I love you,' she repeated as if it were some magic spell that would keep him alive.

'I'll call you when you can see him,' the nurse said, when they had brought him in. 'It will be some little time, I'm afraid. Would you like a cup of tea?'

They gave her tea, very strong and very sweet, and she drank it down not even tasting it. Then she sat waiting for what seemed like hours. At one stage Piet came in and sat quietly beside her, holding her hand.

'You needn't have come, Piet,' she said. 'I can manage alone.'

He sat beside her, hardly speaking but trying to give her some kind of reassurance.

'If he dies,' she said, 'I'll feel it's my fault, just as I felt with Dion.'

'What nonsense,' said Piet. 'How can you say that? And anyhow, he's not going to die.'

'I upset him before the race. I should never have come.'

'That didn't cause the accident. It was that other stupid fool.'

'But maybe he could have avoided it if I hadn't had that scene with him before the race.'

'That's absolute rubbish and you know it. Blake would never want you to take any blame to yourself.

Whatever happens, Blake would say he had done it himself.'

'Yes, he's like that, isn't he? Oh, Piet, why have I always been so proud?' she sighed. 'What harm would it have done to tell him he was the only man in my life? Dion didn't mean anything. Nobody did. Only him.'

'You can see him now for a very few minutes, but the doctor would like to see you first.'

It was the nurse, and Gemma's heart sank. Why did the doctor want to see her except to give her bad news? He's dying, she thought. That's what he's going to tell me.

'Mrs Winfield.'

It sounded strange to be called by that name. She hardly felt she had any right to it. The doctor smiled. Surely he couldn't smile if he was going to give her bad news?

'You look more shocked than the patient. You've had a bad time, haven't you? But now it's all over. Your husband will be all right—a few bruises, very slight concussion. He's a very fortunate man.'

'Are you sure? I can't believe it!'

'Certainly. The X-rays and scans didn't show anything seriously wrong. You'll find he's a bit dazed, but he'll be able to go home tomorrow. There's nothing that a night's rest won't cure. He had a very lucky escape. You can see him now, but don't let him overdo it.'

So nothing had changed, she thought, as she went towards the ward. I thought my life had stopped, and now I find it has to go on. She went towards the bed. Blake looked so strange with a white bandage around his head and his face so pale under the tan.

'Hello, Blake,' she said, and took his hand.

'Gemma—what are you doing here?'

'Why shouldn't I be here? I'm your wife, aren't I?'

'My wife. Of course. Oh, Gemma, if you knew how good that sounds now!'

She looked at him, puzzled. Was he still confused by the crash? she wondered.

'Blake, I've only got a few minutes with you, but I want to get something straight before I go away,' she said. She felt determined. She had made up her mind to speak. 'I want to tell you that I love you. I know it's foolish and that you don't love me in the least. I know how you feel about Trina, but when I thought you had been killed, it came to me that I'd never told you. I won't worry you about it, I'll go away now. It's just that I couldn't bear to leave you now without telling you the truth.'

'But, Gemma, darling Gemma, why did you never tell me this before?'

'You never gave me a chance.'

'Nor you me. The night you left I'd made up my mind to have it out with you.'

'Oh, Blake, there's no need to go into that. I know you wanted to tell me that you needed a separation because Trina was getting her freedom. Trina told me.'

'Trina told you that?'

'Of course. That's why I left. I couldn't bear that you should tell me to go after the night you'd made love to me.'

'And I couldn't bear it that you left me. I realised then just how much you meant to me. Trina came to me asking for advice about her intention to get a divorce. But her divorce has nothing to do with us. She may have thought so, but she knows better now. She's going back to Johannesburg, possibly back to her husband. I made it plain to her that you were the only woman I loved.'

'Oh, Blake, you can't mean that!'

'I intended to tell you the night you left, but then I thought you'd gone because you hated me,' he told her.

'How could you think I hated you? I've always loved you—too much, perhaps. I felt horribly guilty because I felt a love for you that I'd never been able to feel for Dion.'

'It's wonderful to hear you say that,' smiled Blake. 'I love you, Gemma. I've loved you almost since the first moment I set eyes upon you, with your large, innocent blue eyes and your secondhand wedding dress. But Dion was there and I thought you loved him. And even on our wedding night, his ghost came between us.'

'I never loved Dion,' she said. 'I felt guilty after his

death and that's why I had those dreadful nightmares. But, Blake, it's you I love. However hard I tried to fight against it, it was always you.'

'Why ever did you try to fight against it?' he wanted to know.

'I thought you'd married me just for the sake of the farm.'

'I was at fault in that. I should have told you about the condition—but, Gemma, believe me, I would have married you even if it had meant losing the farm altogether.'

'I believe you now,' said Gemma. 'Oh, Blake, what fools we've been! And now you're hurt.'

'Not so hurt that I can't give you a demonstration of what life's going to be like for you from now on.'

'Mrs Winfield!' said the scandalised voice of the nurse. 'It's time for Mr Winfield to have his sleeping tablet.'

Gemma came out of the long kiss to find a nurse, starched and prim, standing at her side.

'I'm coming home tomorrow,' said Blake. 'See that you're there, Gemma. All right, Nurse, I'll take the tablet. I'll need a good night's sleep—I don't expect to get much in future.'

Blushing furiously, Gemma made for the door.

'He's his usual self,' she said to Piet. 'Isn't that wonderful?'

Harlequin® Plus
A WORD ABOUT THE AUTHOR

Gwen Westwood makes her home in Durban, South Africa, in a small house with a long stretch of green lawn. Flowering shrubs such as pink hibiscus abound, along with magenta bougainvillea, purple petrea and wild palms. "No wonder," she smiles, "Wynne May [another Harlequin author] once used our house as her hero's residence!"

Gwen grew up in England's industrial north, met her future husband at Birmingham University and sailed to his native South Africa to be married. She has lived there ever since, traveling extensively throughout the country with her engineer husband and their children.

When the children were grown, Gwen decided to enroll in a journalism class. Gradually she began to see her work published: first a recipe column, then children's books. Feeling the need for a change, she decided to write a romance novel. It was at this time that she attended a talk given by an authority on the meaning of beads used by native Africans. "She told us about the custom of the wife giving her husband a necklace called The Keeper of the Heart," Gwen recalls, "and I thought, *that's the title for my first romantic novel.*"

Keeper of the Heart (Romance #1333) was published in 1969. Since that time, Gwen Westwood has become a favorite author, loved for her well-plotted stories set against exotic backgrounds.

BOOK MATE PLUS®

The perfect companion for all larger books! Use it to hold open cookbooks... or while reading in bed or tub. Books stay open flat, or prop upright on an easellike base... pages turn without removing see-through strap. And pockets for notes and pads let it double as a handy portfolio!

**17" x 11" OPEN.
SNAPS SHUT
TO 8½" x 11".**

**Only $9.95 each —
order yours today!**

Available now. Send your name, address, and zip or postal code, along with a check or money order for just $9.95, plus 75¢ for postage and handling, for a total of $10.70 (New York & Arizona residents add appropriate sales tax) payable to Harlequin Reader Service to:

Harlequin Reader Service

In U.S.
P.O. Box 52040
Phoenix, AZ 85072-9988

In Canada
649 Ontario Street
Stratford, Ont. N5A 6W2

Great old favorites...
Harlequin Classic Library

The **HARLEQUIN CLASSIC LIBRARY**
is offering some of the best in romance fiction—
great old classics from our early publishing lists.
Complete and mail this coupon today!

FREE BONUS BOOK

Harlequin Reader Service

In U.S.A. 1440 South Priest Drive
Tempe, AZ 85281

In Canada 649 Ontario Street
Stratford, Ontario N5A 6W2

Please send me the following novels from the Harlequin Classic Library. I am enclosing my check or money order for $1.50 for each novel ordered, plus 75¢ to cover postage and handling. If I order all nine titles at one time, I will receive a FREE book, *District Nurse*, by Lucy Agnes Hancock.

- ☐ 118 **Then Come Kiss Me**
  Mary Burchell
- ☐ 119 **Towards the Dawn**
  Jane Arbor
- ☐ 120 **Homeward the Heart**
  Elizabeth Hoy
- ☐ 121 **Mayenga Farm**
  Kathryn Blair
- ☐ 122 **Charity Child**
  Sara Seale
- ☐ 123 **Moon at the Full**
  Susan Barrie
- ☐ 124 **Hope for Tomorrow**
  Anne Weale
- ☐ 125 **Desert Doorway**
  Pamela Kent
- ☐ 126 **Whisper of Doubt**
  Andrea Blake

Number of novels checked @ $1.50 each = $ _____
N.Y. and Ariz. residents add appropriate sales tax $ _____
Postage and handling $ ____.75
TOTAL $ _____

I enclose _____
(Please send check or money order. We cannot be responsible for cash sent through the mail.)

Prices subject to change without notice.

Name _____
(Please Print)

Address _____
(Apt. no.)

City _____

State/Prov. _____ Zip/Postal Code _____
Offer expires May 31, 1984

31156000000